PRAISE FOR RUNAWAY TRAIN

"An engaging '90s pastiche with an earnest heart beating at its center."

—Kirkus Reviews

"A mixtape of the 90s, paired with a beautiful story of love, loss, and finding yourself. I couldn't put it down!"
—Raegan Revord, Missy Cooper on TV's
Young Sheldon and founder of the
#ReadingWithRaegan book club

"Raw. Riveting. *Runaway Train* stays true to its title as it explores the deep pain of a teenager desperately trying to find peace in a world full of pain. Lee Matthew Goldberg is a master at bestowing sympathy and strength on deeply flawed characters. Realistic and shocking, hopeful and satisfying, *Runaway Train* will keep readers turning the page."
—*USA Today* Bestselling Author Rebecca Forster

"It's an incredibly challenging task for an author to utilize a darkly comedic tone without coming across as disingenuous—but Goldberg executes it here with expert precision. Brimming over with the visceral atmosphere of the early 90s grunge era, *Runaway Train* is a must-read for those willing to buckle up for the ride."
—Peter Malone Elliott, Book Pipeline

"In *Runaway Train*, Nico takes the leap every teenager dreams of taking, but it's a leap few writers have handled as well as Goldberg. He pulls apart the teen puzzle of feeling both adrift and intentional in the same moment and reminds us that finding a way to be heard is the only way anybody finds themselves."

—Rick Polito, author of *Off Trail*

"All fans of '90s alternative, no matter their generation, will find something to love in this book. A story of a young, drifting woman, who has lost her older sister abruptly and decides, as her family crumbles, to run away, *Runaway Train* presents an adventure, an escape fantasy, and the possibilities of life when you're young and on the margins. This book is a delight for readers of all ages."

—Alex DiFrancesco, author of
All City and *Transmutation: Stories*

"*Runaway Train* is a high-energy testimonial to the redemptive power of a road trip with an awesome soundtrack. Lee Matthew Goldberg balances the urgency of youth with a whiff of anticipatory nostalgia for the music and misadventures of late adolescence. Attuned to way distinctions between music genres and teen idols can feel like impermeable walls worth defending, and then crumble as a teen like Nico Sullivan finds her own voice."

— Jenn Stroud Rossman, author of
The Place You're Supposed to Laugh

VANISH ME

A RUNAWAY TRAIN NOVEL

• • • • • • • •

VANISH ME

• • • • • • • •

LEE MATTHEW GOLDBERG

 WISE WOLF BOOKS 🐾 LAS VEGAS

WISE WOLF
BOOKS

VANISH ME. Copyright © 2022 by Lee Matthew Goldberg. All rights reserved.

For information, address Wolfpack Publishing, 5130 S. Fort Apache Road, 215-380 Las Vegas, NV 89148

wisewolfbooks.com

Cover design by Wise Wolf Books

Paperback ISBN 978-1-953944-21-4
eBook ISBN 978-1-953944-68-9
LCCN 2021952566

First Edition: February 2022

TO THE MUSIC THAT'S A SOUNDTRACK

FOR OUR LIVES

"I am disappearing, maybe I'm already gone."

– Jennifer Niven, All the Bright Places

SOMEDAY IN 1998

• • • • •

Drown - Smashing Pumpkins

I gave birth twice this year: to Evanico, the band, and my daughter Love. Neither feels real. Evanico came first, a union. Evan and I back in love, together again, bursting to make art. Neither of us able to exist without music seeping from our pores. A guitar like a security blanket slung across his shoulder. The echo of a song turning me whole. We left Grenade Bouquets a simmering pile of ash and became reborn in a small house in Eugene, Oregon with a tiny cat we called Dave Grohl. We swore to keep the music we created for ourselves, but that was foolish. A run-in outside of a club with Courtney Love would change all that. She'd hear me sing a song called "Winter" and tell me to send it to her record company. Even though I knew Evan would be pissed, I pulled out the pin in that grenade and gave it a whirl.

He'd come around. Slowly at first, skeptical, hiding behind the thick blond hair he'd grown so long till the ends touched his lips. We had a knock-down, drag-out fight on the way to meet with the executives, expecting a scenario filled with sharks like we had with Grouch Records, but this was different. Astral Records, named after Van Morrison's "Astral Weeks"—it helped we had a homey version of "The Way That Young Lovers Do", over a glockenspiel—was chasing a Lilith Fair sound to compete with the new titans of the industry: Sarah McLachlan, Fiona Apple, Sheryl Crow, Jewel. Women fronted bands were finally in and we'd help usher this revolution. Grunge had expired, the Grenade Bouquets had broken at the wrong time, but we hadn't been *so* well-known that we couldn't have a second act.

"Take the time to record an album," the record people said, nodding like bobbleheads. "'Winter' will be the star of the album but think of it like a planet. Create the entire universe."

These execs weren't sleazy men with accents that veered depending on their moods. They were women in flowing dresses, men raised by single mothers. They cared for our wellbeing. Wanted to nurture us, make us flowers. We were their seeds.

And Evan and I relished this soft sell. They got a studio in Eugene, so we didn't have to leave, set us up with one of the best sound engineers in the business, and every day we brought Dave Grohl into our recording booth and didn't leave until the middle of the night. We'd emerge, wiped-out but vibrating, our little family. My parents had long given up on me getting a G.E.D. and supported us. They'd grown to love Evan like I did, visiting once we finished laying down tracks for a low-key set we played at Café Hey. I think back and that was the happiest I'd ever been. Winter and Jeremy and Aunt Carly there too. Everyone I cared about the most in one room as we played "Winter" and cried a little, although they were smiley tears.

And then: the inevitable. The album took off. And I mean, rocketed to the moon. Evanico was everywhere. *Rolling Stone, Spin,* rotation on MTV, huge tours all over the world. Four singles were released, each one outdoing the next. We were invited to Lilith Fair and Lollapalooza. The year passed by in a blur. Evan and I spent so much time together that we didn't exist as a couple anymore. We were Evanico, unified only by chords, and we could barely muster up the enthusiasm to be more. Astral wanted a second album, but we lacked the juice. We had lost ourselves. Everything we did was for the masses. If I took a shit, I sometimes wondered if I had to ask my publicist if it was ok. We were shiny versions of the Evan and Nico we once were, but deep down we were screaming. Dave Grohl developed a weird type of cancer and died, and we found ourselves in each other's arms. It had been a while since we'd had sex, even slept in the same bed. We'd left Eugene because Astral put us up in a glorious house in L.A. that overlooked the hills. After burying Dave Grohl in the front yard, we dropped ecstasy because it was in at the time and that's what Dave Grohl would've wanted us to do. Out of our gourds, we had sex one night on our terrace to Smashing Pumpkins' "Drown" with the L.A. smog making the sky a pinkish purple. I was so thirsty, not realizing it was from the E, believing Evan could satisfy my emptiness.

A few weeks later in Europe, I couldn't make it through a morning without puking, so I saw a doctor.

I pegged it as stress, maybe depression, since I realized I was glummer than the average girl, but nope, I was knocked-up. I'd thought of myself as pro-choice, but when it came to my own body, I couldn't. My parents steered me toward a Planet Parenthood clinic, swearing that my life was "just starting" and it would be "impossible to tour with a baby at my breast," (thank my mother for those words of wisdom). Winter and Jeremy said "I'd lose my body and get saggy". Astral said basically that same thing in a more polite way. Even Evan, sweet Evan, who left the choice entirely up to me, but every once in a while, would check in to make sure I was making the right decision. I knew it freaked him the fuck out to be a father at twenty-one, myself only nineteen. But then I'd picture this little nugget in my arms, this little nugget I'd just have to love for the rest of my life. What if this was my only chance at being a mom? I knew I would regret getting rid of the child more than I ever would keeping it, so that gave me the answer I needed.

Love Marvin was born on Halloween 1997, eight pounds, two ounces with her fat cherub face and peach fuzz blonde hair. She was perfect, and I wanted to be perfect for her. But I was far from it.

I'd have trouble getting out of bed. Love would cry and I'd block out my ears. I'd feel like a machine to her, since all I could do was feed until my breasts were sore. Feed and sleep. Feed and sleep. Evan took care of everything, a hero. I was a milk factory and other than that, a disappointment. I was drowning. Life was a series of moving through water, a slow-motion torture chamber. I loved Love; I knew I did, but she disgusted me as well. I know that's terrible to say, but it was the truth. Evan could barely look at me, even more disgusted. Motherhood brought out my true self, a cipher. So, I left. One morning while she cried and Evan rushed to catch her tears—he was always rushing after her, as if each cry meant she was dying—I took a hit from a roach at the bedstand, threw some Lilith Fair-esque floral dresses in a beat-up suitcase, grabbed the car keys, and disappeared. Left in the same car I first ran away with when I was a child, even though I really hadn't grown. I still had a longing festering inside of me that fame, fortune, motherhood, or true love couldn't squelch.

I had no idea where I was going; all I knew was that I had to get their fast, speeding down highways with spinning sirens eating my dust.

Someday, they'd tell the story of my ghost, this girl named Nico made up of air and mist, who vanished from everyone with the goal of vanishing from the person she most wanted to get away from—herself.

1

• • • • •

NOTHINGMAN – PEARL JAM

2014

"Love!"

Somewhere in another realm I think I hear my name. I'm in bed, headphones on, listening to Lit's "My Own Worst Enemy". While not grunge per se—my true love—I've been working through each year's alternative rock charts beginning with 1991 and pretty proud of myself that I'm already at 1997. Having a meager social life certainly helps.

My dad bursts in the door. Shit, I hadn't locked it. "Love!"

He looks bewildered, classic Dad. His long blond hair now with echoes of grey. A flesh-colored beard that eats up his face. And ugh, Frankie and Caden, my two besties, would still call him a DILF because they know it pisses me off. Caden has two moms, and Frankie's dad was never in the picture, so there isn't much competition.

"I was asking what you wanted for dinner," he says, flipping that hair out of his eyes. Something he does when he's exasperated. "Marjorie's joining us."

Marjorie. A perfectly harmless woman. Marjorie owns the bakery down the block from Café Hey, where my dad likes to hang and occasionally play sets. That's how they met. She was on her lunch break eating a blondie at Café Hey, my dad asked if they made good blondies, and she replied she made them herself. He was instantly smitten.

So, they've been dating about four months, but a family dinner is new territory. Dad dated a lot, I mean, a lot for a dad, but the women usually never made it past four months. I worry Marjorie's time is about to be up.

"I was thinking—I don't know…" He gives a hair flip that's pointless because it goes right back in his eyes. "Pasta. Do people still eat pasta?"

I place my Sports Walkman to the side—this conversation would stretch a little longer. And yes, I have a Sports Walkman. It's my treasure. It's yellow and huge and plays all my favorite mixtapes. Fuck Spotify and Pandora and any other streaming service. I don't even have a smart phone. I live like the cave people did, or at least how people in the 90s did. I have a budget flip-phone like a drug dealer, only for emergencies and have never participated in social media. Spoiler: no one gives a donkey's balls about every little thing you do all day. Frankie and Caden feel the same and we've dubbed our crew 9021-*Hole*, after two of our fav 90's cultural touchstones. *90210* and, I mean, I was named after Hole's lead singer.

"No one eats pasta anymore," I say. "At least not gluten pasta. Do you have quinoa?"

"Every time I make it, it comes out clumpy."

I slide out of bed. "I'll do it. Remind me, Marjorie's allergic to mushrooms?"

"Right, she'll die."

"So, extra shitake?"

I hop downstairs on our rickety steps. Honestly, the whole house in is disrepair and likely haunted, but I love that it's decrepit. It was the first house my parents lived in a thousand years ago when they were still in love and made an album that's pretty rocking and awesome in a makes-you-wanna-sway-with-your-lighter. Mom—well she peaced out when I was just a squirt and returned only in fits and spurts. Sometimes I hear of her trapsing around in France, and once in a blue moon, I'll get a postcard. She has a weird loopy penmanship, and not to sound like a sap, but I keep everything she sends.

When she comes into town, it's only to see me. It's not that she hates Dad, far from it; she's afraid he never got over her, and that's the truth. In the middle of the night, I've heard him on the porch strumming "The Way That Young Lovers Do", his voice wavering, which lets me know he's been crying. I've heard you never get over your first love, but I wouldn't know because at sixteen, the most I've done is kissed a boy. He attacked me with his slobbery tongue, so I'm not rushing for that to happen again.

I catch myself in the mirror on the way down the stairs. My blonde hair kept perfectly messy, a plaid flannel shirt, Doc Martens, a face like the cutest chipmunk you've ever known. I'm a spitting image of my mom at my age. I've seen pictures of her, and it's given me goosebumps. I know it's hard for my dad to see me at times, but like, this is who I am. You can psychoanalyze me all you want and TRUST, I've been through that. I know I retreat to the '90s to find some closeness with my mom since she's not around, but it makes me happy. I was literally born in the wrong century and there's nothin' I can do about it but bathe in nostalgia.

In the kitchen, I get out the quinoa, start to boil the water. Cut up tomatoes and zucchini that I roast with coconut oil. Dad comes down in his tucked-in checkered shirt and uncool tie. He must've had a class earlier today. He teaches music theory over at the University of Oregon and has invited his students over for jam sessions before. They get stars in their eyes because he once was famous, and all the young ladies swoon. I want to barf.

"How's school?" he asks, doing this check-in once a week or so.

I take out a block of Parmesan cheese to cut up in the quinoa. "Crappy."

"You always say that."

"Then maybe stop asking."

We're silent and then I laugh to show I'm just joking. As dads go, he's a pretty great one, and look, he raised me as a single parent and treats me like I'm the second coming of Christ, so I can't really give him too much shit.

He swipes some OJ from the fridge and takes a sip. "Maybe if you joined some clubs?"

"Gross, Dad." I slam a cup on the counter. "Put

it in a glass. And did *you* join any clubs in school?"

"Well, no…"

"You got stoned and played guitar in your room. Full stop."

"I was in a band."

"Before Grenade Bouquets?"

I stop, those words *verboten*. He gives me a lingering look.

"Yeah, we were called The Dead Skies."

"The Dead Skies?" I mime retching.

"The lead singer Duke and I fought over a girl and that ended our reign."

"Probably for the best."

The water boils and I toss in the quinoa, wait for the little orbs to grow plump. We both are vegetarian, so meat has never graced our fridge.

"What time is Marjorie coming?" I ask.

He looks at his dorky Casio watch. "Shit, I need to shower."

"Yeah, tell me about it."

"Funny," he says, kissing me on the top of my head. I pretend like I'm grossed out, but really, it's sweet. "Thank you for making dinner."

"My pleasure, anything to keep Marjorie around."

He stops at the foot of the stairs, cocks his head. "I didn't realize you liked her that much."

"I don't, but I like *you* with her, so just working my magic like I do."

He chews on the side of his cheek. "I don't deserve you, do I?"

"Nope. So, maybe an increase in my allowance?" I bat my eyes.

"Capitalist," he says, swinging up the stairs.

The quinoa has turned plump, so I strain out the water before it gets too clumpy. Upstairs, I hear him singing Pearl Jam's "Nothingman" in our shower.

"Nothingman," he sings. "Fuck, shit, damn," as I can tell the water pressure is turning from hot to cold. A jolt I know all too well. "Caught a bolt of lightning, cursed the day he let it go. Oh, oh, oh. Nothingmaaaaaaaan."

2

• • • • •

DESPERATELY WANTING – BETTER THAN EZRA

Nothing excites me more than Finals Week because school is finally O-V-E-R. The shitshow that's been junior year will no longer be spoken about—and honestly, there really isn't much to say. It mostly consisted of Frankie, Caden and I avoiding everyone like they contracted leprosy. Roam the halls and find everyone with a third arm (their phone). Everything was Facebook this, or Instagram that, even Snapchat was starting to gain traction, whatever the funk that was. Had we all created this new Medusa whose social media head would get lopped off only for another to take its place. No thank you, ma'am.

So, it's refreshing to see Frankie and Caden by their lockers with zero third arms. They're sharing headphones and I come up from behind and give a listen, "Desperately Wanting" by Better Than Ezra, a late post-grunge track.

"Hey, Love," they say in unison. They have a tendency to do that, speak as one. Or, more so, Caden is glued to Frankie, and she bathes in the attention.

Frankie is wearing a heavy flannel even though it's June, causing her shoulders to droop. She's sans make-up like usual, her hair barely combed, wild and free. She's got Doc Martins because that's our thing. We wear 'em until the soles fall off. Caden is pretty much dressed the same, his hair dyed auburn, an eyebrow ring sparkling.

"Hey, hey," I say, doing a tah-dah tap dance. "Two more finals to go and then I'm dunzo."

"I still have Spanish," Frankie says. "*No me gusta.* I'm like, the worst in the class. Which is crazy because I'm *half* Spanish."

"What about that guy who eats paint chips?" I ask.

"Paint Chip Peter? *He's* even doing better than me. If I have to go to summer school—"

"You won't," Caden says. Caden's quiet, at least compared to Frankie and I; two motormouths who'll eat up the air in a room. Well, a room with the three of us at least.

"Seriously, our summer is set," I say. "We're gonna listen to every post-grunge song of 1997 and beyond and see which of those bands might be coming through Eugene."

"*No one* comes through Eugene," Frankie says.

"Some of these bands haven't had a hit since then, so they should be happy to play here."

"Maybe your dad could do a set with one of them?" Caden says, his eyes swimming on the filthy floor.

I punch him in the shoulder. "Ugh, gag me with a spoon. Speaking of Dad, Marjorie came over for dinner last night."

"Oooohhhhh dinner," they both said. "Means it's serious," Frankie adds.

Frankie does this thing where she twitches her nose when she's being mischievous. It's super cute and makes her look like a bunny.

"I made them quinoa."

"Bringing out the big guns," Caden says, giving the same nervous laugh he does anytime he makes a joke.

"More like the big grains," Frankie says, which makes Caden giggle even more like we're tickling his belly.

Two meathead jocks run past, practically knocking us all over. They're punching each other, whooping it up—the animals. The least attractive person on the planet is someone who devotes their life to sports.

Frankie spins around, fixing her glasses that have gone askew, and gives them the finger. "Watch it, Gym Socks."

"It's the Ghosts," one meathead says in the other's ear. "So invisible they might as well be ghosts."

This gets them guffawing, their energy turning dangerous. One shuffles over and knocks Caden's Walkman to the ground.

"What the fuck is that even?" the meathead says, pointing to the cracked device.

"It *was* a Walkman, you asshole," Frankie says, pushing him hard enough into the wall that the guy almost falls. Don't mess with Frankie.

"Huh huh, whatever, Ghost."

He gets his buddy into a headlock, and they're gone. Caden has tears in his eyes, so sensitive. He picks it up and hesitantly pushes play. The faint sound of Better Than Ezra can still be heard.

"They deserve Ex-Lax in their cereals," Frankie says, and Caden cracks a smile. "Two more days and we won't have to think of them until September."

This is why there wasn't much about this year to remember. If it wasn't the meatheads bothering us, or the popular posse of girls that ignored us—which was worse; we really were ghosts. Come senior year, grace through the pages of the yearbook and people would be like, yeah, that girl Love, the one with the weird name, I think she was in my Bio class. I don't know, she'd fade into the background.

I grabbed Caden's headphones, the song "Desperately Wanting" against my ear. What was it that I wanted? I couldn't even think of anything I really desired except listening to music, and maybe hanging out with my mom more. It had been a long time since I'd seen her. The last time we went to Portland, we saw this band her friend was in—they were hippie dippie, but pretty cool. We waited on-line forever at Voodoo Donuts, munched them on the hood of her car. She didn't talk much, and I found myself asking most of the questions.

"Where are you living now?"

She replied with a gesture of her hands, seemingly living everywhere.

"What are you doing for work?"

With donut mush in her mouth, she mumbled something that sounded like "tech".

"Why did you leave me?"

This I never asked, even though I wanted to. It risked

the chance of her ever returning.

Like a cruel witch, she held that spell over me.

"What'd you think of the band?" she asked, after a bout of silence.

I shrugged my shoulders, crammed in another donut. "They were okay I guess?"

"Yeah, Lane was a little pitchy," she said, shielding her eyes from the sun. "Everyone's a little pitchy these days."

"I'm up to 1996," I said, referring to the grunge playlist I was barreling through, but she didn't hear, or didn't care.

We got back in her old sputtering car, one with knobs for the radio while she searched for a song. One I never heard before popped up, throaty and sounding like it came from a long-ago time. She sang along softly, always softly now, her voice riddled from cigarettes and booze, two vices I swore never to partake. She sang so quiet I had to lean in to listen. That was all the music anyone would get from her anymore. From old fans, even her only daughter. The past had harmed her too much to tap into what she used to love. Although that past remained a mystery to us all. Maybe the thing I craved more than anything else was that I desperately wanted to know her story.

The song ends and Caden takes back his headphones, tucks his chin into his neck so he appears smaller—this shy ball of a boy. We all agree to meet at my place after school and celebrate finishing our finals. Maybe watch some old episodes of *90210*—certainly not the reboot. I once read a letter from my mom that likened herself to Brenda from the show, so I like to think I'm the same.

As I leave them, I see Frankie tracing circles around Caden's back. He's still upset, and I love how nurturing Frankie can be. I want to shout across the halls that I could use some nurturing too, but the bell rings and chaos erupts. Like the ghost they bill me as, I slink between the crowd unnoticed to head to an algebra final where I'll likely do not much better than average.

3

• • • • •

NEVER THERE – CAKE

After bombing my algebra and likely my US history finals, I'm officially dunzo with school for the semester. So, Frankie, Caden and I are Audi 5000. For my sixteenth birthday, I'd been blessed with a license and a used car from my dad, which gave us the freedom to avoid the school bus. Thank Jesus for that. The meatheads rule the bus with their beer can brains and we'd be subjected to more of their insults. It pisses me off that Frankie's the only one with enough guts to stand up to them. I stood there mute as always. In my mind, I'm a hero with a demolishing tongue. In reality, I'm no better than Caden: a quiet mouse that enjoys finding walls to blend into. I know I'm a good chunk responsible for our trio to be labeled as Ghosts.

But in my beat-up dark-blue Honda Accord with a Gods-Eye hanging from the rearview and almost a hundred thousand miles logged on the odometer (mostly from the previous owner), I'm whoever I want to be. With Frankie sitting shotgun and Caden in the back, we crank up tunes, Cake's "Never There", and sing out of the windows. School's not far from home, so it's only about a fifteen-minute drive, but I'm freer in those fifteen minutes at the end of each day than during the rest of my existence. Caden's tapping on the back of the seat, Frankie's terrible (but loveable) voice screams the chorus, and I'm grooving. I think of my mom only for a second—how I've never really, *truly* heard her sing—and then toss her out of my mind. I'll be damned if she ruins the rest of my day.

Back at home, we convene in my room surrounded by posters of grunge gods: Cobain, Love, Vedder, Weiland, Cornell, Corgan. My desk full of stacked CDs. The benefit of being so into a type of music twenty-something years after the fact is that it comes pretty cheap. There's a used record store in town and most CDs are .99 cents. I work a couple of shifts at the barista counter at Café Hey a few days a week and coupled with my twenty-dollar allowance, I'm swimming in all the music I want.

We take out the Big Notebook and add "Never There" to the list. Our goal is to listen to every grunge and post-grunge song that made the top one hundred of each year. I write in the Cake song and highlight it, meaning it's a track I dug and want to get the CD.

Caden has his Sports Walkman out. He's stopping the tape and rewinding and it's making a weird sound.

"It's not broken, but something's definitely up." He sighs with the weight of the world and picks at his eyebrow ring.

"Those shitknobs should pay for it…somehow," Frankie says, rubbing her hands together, and I get a nervous ball in my stomach. Frankie has a habit of going *way* too far when she messes with people.

"Forget it," I say, trying to change the subject. "*90210* marathon?"

Frankie flops back on the bed, zips off her Doc Martins. Her socks have holes in them and one toe that's painted lavender bursts through. I catch Caden eyeing it too, and he catches me doing the same before we both nervously look away.

"Is your dad home?" Caden asks, a way of diverting the conversation.

"Uh, I dunno." I peer outside the window to see if Dad's car is parked out front, but no dice. "Why?"

"No reason," Caden shrugs while Frankie flips through my CDs and finds some Violent Femmes. She's moving to "Blister in the Sun", swaying her hips, dancing with abandon. I wish I could be more like her. Carefree. It's not like she doesn't have worries like we all do; she just won't let them drag her down. Like with her mom who has issues. She never got over Frankie's father leaving, kinda like with my dad, but her mom is way sadder about it. Sometimes she doesn't leave the house and Frankie has to do all the shopping. Frankie won't really talk about it too much.

"I see your dad," Caden says, pointing at a car pulling up outside.

"Okay, chill, it's not like we doing anything bad."

Caden's always been a little obsessed with my dad. He makes him nervous, and I don't exactly know why. I know his two moms are the best and really love him, but he has no men in his life, no uncles, no guy friends, just me and Frankie. So, I think my dad has become this like male role model to him, and Caden always wants to be on his absolute best behavior.

When I look out of the window, Dad's running from his car into the house. His eyes are bugging, and he moves with a purpose, clearly upset. I scroll through my brain if I might be the cause of his agitation. Besides my toilet grades, there's nothing bad I could remember doing and it's not like he'd find out about my finals before I did.

Caden picks more at his eyebrow ring. "He looks mad."

"You mean the DILF?" Frankie says, her smile stretching wide. "Oh, Mr. Marvin, could we go over some music theory?"

"Stop," I say, as Caden's nervous laugh starts up.

We hear Dad bounding up the stairs. I swallow my heart as the door flings open.

"Love—" he stammers, seeing Frankie dancing and Caden twiddling his thumbs. "Oh, I didn't realize you had... I should have known your friends were over."

"Yeah, because they're pretty much over every day," I say.

Frankie bounces over. "It's true we should pay you some rent, Evan."

I hate when she calls my dad by his first name.

"I have to talk to Love," he says, not even bothering to be nice about it.

"Dad!" I squeal. "That's so rude. You can say anything in front of them."

His face morphs, pleading now. "Please, kids... Love will see you tomorrow."

"Dad, we're celebrating finals being over—"

"Now, Love, I'm *serious*."

I jump a little because he shouts, which he never does. Frankie and Caden get the hint and give me a quick hug as they depart. Frankie makes a call me sign at the door before she shuts it closed.

"Dad, what's going—"

"I'm sorry," he says, running his fingers through his hair, getting them caught in its knots. "It's your mom…"

Now my stomach really drops. I'm on a rollercoaster ticking away to the top about to go over the edge. My whole life I've dreaded hearing bad news about my mom. That she drank too much or had taken a drug she shouldn't have. That she got herself in a terrible situation she couldn't worm her way out of.

My eyes water, waiting to burst. "Is she…?"

"She's missing."

I recalibrate, let out a stifled breath.

"Yes, missing. She—was in France. Nice. I got a call from her landlady. She hasn't been there in a while."

"Maybe she's traveling?"

"The rent is overdue by two months."

"Wait, how did her landlady know to call you?"

"I co-sign her rent."

I tug on my lip with my teeth, digging in. "I didn't know you guys were in touch." A dot of blood teases my tongue.

"We're not, I mean, just about this. She called me earlier this year, said she needed help with some money issues."

"She didn't ask to speak to me?"

Now the waterworks flow. While I always felt bad

about my parents' strained relationship, a part of me enjoyed being the one my mom cared about more. But here she had called, and I wasn't even a thought? I hug my legs up to my chin.

"You haven't gotten any new postcards?" he asks.

"No, nothing. The last time I saw her was in the fall when we went to that show in Portland."

"Right, right."

I remember how awkward that had been. Mom idling in the car outside while I went down, and Dad watched from the window like a stalker. When I got home, he couldn't even ask how it was, just grabbed his guitar and retreated to his bedroom to pluck.

"I even contacted her folks," Dad says, tugging at his hair now.

"Grandma Luanne and Grandpa Peter?"

It'd been a few years since I'd see them last. For my birthday, they always call and send a card. They each live with different spouses and probably haven't been in touch with my mom since Y2K. Both are in L.A. and hanging out with them was…weird. It's like they were searching for my mom in me, unhappy with this version of her.

"They didn't hear from her either."

"She's never been close with them."

"Grandpa Peter has…well, some health issues, Love."

"You never told me that!"

"I didn't want to upset… Anyway, your mom knows about her father, so she's been in touch more."

Again, a stab of jealousy wiggles through my bloodstream. "Really?"

"She's been checking in with him once in a while. He's…I mean, he'll likely be okay. Cancer, but in remission."

"Oh…" I say, sounding so small and far away. I'm feeling like I'm not a part of this family at all.

"With school, we just didn't want to worry you about him, and he's…he's really going to be okay, but the fact that she hasn't checked in in over two months, with anyone… It's not good."

"No."

"No, it isn't. I'm gonna…make some calls, the police in Nice."

"Oh, jeez."

He steps closer and holds out his arms to hug. I fold into his lean body, unsure who is comforting who. Our shared worry vibrates between us.

"Okay," he says, pulling away and wiping a sleeve across his bloodshot eyes.

"What can I do?" I ask, feeling more helpless than I ever have before.

"Maybe, just order a pizza. I don't know…"

He goes to the door, his hand on the knob.

"Dad?"

He stops. "Yeah?"

"I'm scared."

"Me…me, too."

And then he's gone, and I'm left all alone. The world seeming super big, too many pockets for a soul like my mother to lose herself, whether by choice or by being in the wrong place at the wrong time.

I'm humming "Never There", over and over. *You're never, never, never, never there*, my new psalm, as if

I keep humming it, I can reverse this course of reality and make her reappear again, at my door in her long hippie skirt and sandals, her hair smelling of the beach, a lipstick kiss left on my cheek as a reminder not to forget her because the memory may be all we have.

4

• • • • •

MOTHER MOTHER – TRACY BONHAM

While Dad makes some calls and we wait for the pizza to arrive, I go up to the dusty attic to pilfer through a box of my mom's old things. Since she never had a permanent home, she chose to keep it all safe here. Some are artifacts from her teen years: an alien midi ring, warped Sassy magazines ("Ten Ways to Dress with a Flannel Other Than as a Shirt"), stubs from a Grenade Bouquets show, a mixtape called "Runaway Train" with that song as the third track, handwritten lyrics for "Ready To Guide" written in purple pen that I heard was about her sister, my Aunt Kristen, who died long before I ever existed. And then, at the bottom of the box, while I sniffle, I pull out what looks like a diary I've never noticed before. *Believe* me, I've obsessively studied every object in here, so it's baffling to think I could've missed a jackpot into my mom's psyche.

The pages are worn, dark pen used on both sides. Flipping through, some of them have photos taped inside as well. On the cover, a hand drawn picture of a boy and a girl's face in marker, their lips an inch apart, mouths reaching toward one another. A chill tickles down my spine. Did my mom leave this for me? Did she know she was about to vanish for good and this would be a memento to remember her? To attempt to get to know her better? My fingers shake as I turn to the first page. A Polaroid photo pops out. It's her band Grenade Bouquets in front of a VW van with the hot sun bathing them yellow. I notice my mom right away because she looks just like me, except she has blue hair. She's staring at the camera, her eyes peering into my soul. She's smiling and making a rock sign with her hand, but she seems spooked—like she has no idea who she is or how she got to be in this photo. Like the camera has stolen her innocence.

Next to her, Dad has his thin arm wrapped around her neck, giving a sweet smile. His hair so blond it looks fake, this mini Kurt Cobain in a striped green wool sweater that he still knocks around the house in from time to time. I think of all they were doing with their lives when they were basically my age—about to go on tour and take over the world for a moment where I could barely keep up a C average in school, no ambition, no calling like they had. I hate to admit I'm embarrassed for myself.

I go over to the window, since the attic is dark, and I can only read from a slit of light filtering inside. I'm nervous like I'm being let in on a secret I shouldn't know, opening this door to my mom that might unlock all my questions. Not only where she might have gone, but who she really is. And more than that, is she someone I even want to know?

"Love," I hear faintly from the floor below. It's my dad. "Pizza's here."

"I'll take it in my room," I yell back.

Something tells me I shouldn't show him this diary. That my mom knew the attic was a place I retreated to and he never did. This clue meant for me alone. I head down the ladder, the diary close to my chest. He's on his cell, gesturing for me to come to the kitchen. I swipe a slice of green pepper and onion, slap it on a paper plate, and scurry to my bedroom. Sitting criss-cross-apple-sauce on my bed, I stretch the cheese with my teeth and take a deep, deep breath when my flip-phone rings. It's Frankie, so I answer.

"Hey, you okay"?" she asks, and I feel more settled than I did a few seconds ago. Her voice has the power to do that.

"Yeah, it's my mom. She's like missing."

I go into the whole story, my voice cracking. She listens like a best friend.

"I'm sure she's okay," Frankie says, even though there's no way to be sure. Her mom has disappeared before. Sometimes wandering through Eugene in her nightgown in the middle of the night. This is only when she overdoes it on her meds.

"I know you get it," I say, and I hear Frankie whistling.

"I mean, yeah, like both our moms are space cases. Sometimes it's like I'm the mom."

"Yeah. Totally."

I reach over and pick through my CDs, landing on Tracy Bonham's "Mother Mother". Tracy looking badass in a sleeveless top in front of a brick wall.

"I found her diary in the attic," I say.

"Whoa, what does it say?"

"I haven't read it yet. But like, I never noticed it in her box of things, and I've gone through that box before."

"Wow, that's super intense. You think she left it for you?"

"Dunno," I say, putting the Tracy Bonham CD into my old Aiwa stereo, hitting play, and keeping it on a low volume. "But I'm about to find out."

"Gimme all the deets at school tomorrow, Love. And good luck. Whatever you need me for, I'm there."

There are things I want to tell her that I haven't gotten up the courage to say, that I don't even know how to put into words, or how I really feel, so I thank her and hang up.

I take another bite of pizza, crank up "Mother Mother", and turn the first page to an entry marked, September 30th, 1996 – *Love Buzz – Nirvana*.

5

• • • • •

LOVE BUZZ – NIRVANA

September 30th, 1996

I drive to Eugene, Oregon after mailing the song "Winter" that Evan and I created with our new band, Evanico. Soon Courtney Love's record company will give it a listen and decide our future. But the future I'm more concerned about is with Evan. I repeat this to myself over and over. I start my journey with Soundgarden's "Blow Up the Outside World" and reach Eugene deep into the night, eyes bleary, with the fuzz of Nirvana's "Love Buzz" pouring from my windows.

When I go inside, Evan sits on the couch with our kitty Dave Grohl and I dive into his arms. I stay hugging him without saying much, Dave Grohl cuddling between us. We have both been through a lot. He was in Idaho with his family where his brother had to be checked into a facility, and I'd come from my sister's grave. Her ghost had given me the sign I needed in the form of the wind to take the chance and send our tape to Courtney Love's people. Evan wants to keep us small, playing tiny sets at coffee shops, focusing on us as a couple. But I honestly have the drive once again to take over the world.

We go to bed, both of us wanting sex, a connection, but too tired to move our limbs in the right way. I sleep hard, no dreams, and when I wake, I smell eggs coming from the kitchen and find Evan in an apron that says "Dis The Cook". He's whipping up eggs and bacon and my stomach growls like the pissed off monster it is.

"It's almost noon," he says, tickling Dave Grohl under the chin, who weaves across the counter. "I tried to wake you, but you were like, not having it. Dead to the world."

"Yeah, I was super tired and still am. How did it go with your brother?"

He stops tickling Dave Grohl, his eyes growing heavy. "I mean, not good. Not a disaster of epic proportions, but he didn't want to be there."

I swipe a mug and pour myself some steaming coffee. "I'm sorry."

"The place really isn't so bad, though. That's a plus. They try to keep them active, but then it's kind of like they're treating them like children. I don't know, it made me really sad."

"And your folks?"

"It's about a twenty-minute drive from them so they'll visit every day. It's better. If he starts getting fits, the place will be able to control him more than they could at home." He holds out a mug. "Hit me with that, I need it bad."

I want to tell him right away about what happened with Courtney Love, but not sure it's the right time. But will any time be the right one? From my experience with life so far, there's always something making a stink.

"Hey, I need to talk to you."

Dave Grohl gives me a look like he knows this isn't gonna be good.

Evan spins over and kisses me on the top of my head. "Ok, is everything all right?"

"Yeah, I mean, it's good news. Really."

He spatulas the eggs onto two separate plates and sits down at the kitchen table with me. His eyes glance up like he's ready for whatever it will be.

"Okay, so, I met Courtney Love..."

"What? Nico, when did that happen?"

"At this club the night of my eighteenth birthday—"

"We talked that night, you never told me!"

"So, I'm outside of this club singing 'Winter', like, and she hears me and she's all, cool song."

"What? This is crazy."

"Crazy good, right?"

He spears his eggs and starts eating. "What did she say?"

"She loved the song, my voice too. We shared a cigarette and talked, it was unreal, like I think I left my body. Anyway, she knew who I was."

"Shut up. She *knew* Grenade Bouquets?"

"Yeah, and thought we were rad, or whatever word she used, I don't remember. She thought I was badass and so..."

The news hangs on my tongue, waiting, waiting...

My stomach twisting, twisting...

"She said to send it to her record company."

He puts his fork down, crosses his arms.

"Nico, we talked about—"

"We *talked* about not working with Grouch Records ever again because of their sketchiness."

"No." He stands with his plate and tosses it in the sink, even though he hasn't finished his eggs. "We decided our relationship is more important than fame."

I join him by the sink, my hand on his back. "Evan, you mean more to me than anything, but why does it have to be one or the other?"

"You saw what happened to us in the Bouquets."

"That was different! We had the rest of the band bringing us down. This is just the two of us—"

"And a record company looking to bleed us dry."

"Maybe not this time. I mean, they rep Hole, they can't be so bad."

He gives a look like he's not buying what I'm slinging.

"Why don't we see what happens before we make a definite decision. If they really like the music, how can we say no?"

He wraps his arms around me, squeezing tight. "Because it might mean losing you."

And then, I say something more adult than I ever have: "If that causes us to break up, we're likely headed in that direction anyway."

He lets go, his touch cold now. It's September and there's a chill in the air. I'm afraid this is a moment we'll never come back from. But what was I supposed to do? Stay silent forever about how I really feel? That couldn't be healthy for a relationship.

"So, Courtney Love really called us rad?"

He's giving that smirk he does, which turns me into melted cheese.

"I forget what actual word she used, but yeah, basically."

He scoops up Dave Grohl. "What do you think, kitty?"

Dave Grohl meows in response.

"I think he said to give it a shot," I say, poking Evan in the spleen.

"He is a wise cat," Evan says.

"Are you mad?"

"No, I can't stay mad at you." He puts Dave Grohl down to hug me again, and I feel safe. "But whatever happens, we really talk it out. No decisions until we both completely agree. Fair?"

I hold out my pinky. "Pinky swear."

We loop fingers. "Pinky swear."

Later that day, we made love to "Love Buzz": the twang of the guitar, the thrashing chords, Cobain's early growl, and the sensation that we were about to soar, again, but this time to heights we couldn't even imagine, buzzing with screaming anticipation.

6

• • • • •

CALIFORNICATION – RED HOT CHILI PEPPERS

The last day of school is a joke. We're there to get our final grades and watch everyone take a zillion pics and videos of themselves. I see people who never really hung out, arm-in-arm, giving peace signs and kissy faces toward the cameras. Last minute friendships to document across platforms, promises to stay in touch over the boiling summer, talk of parties in the woods that I'd never be invited to (not that I'd go). It makes me want to a destroy the cell tower in the area and force them to interact like *actual* individuals and not social media avatars.

Anyway, I'm in a mood in case you can't tell. I have my mom's diary tucked under my arm, not even caring about my posted grades. Frankie and Caden wander over in the hallway by our lockers while morons whoop around us. My ears are assaulted, and I give a *woosah* like my Great Aunt Carly always tells me to do. She lives in Ojai, California with a house full of crystals and cats, the definition of eternally chill.

Frankie looks good as always, wearing a distressed Ramones T-shirt that's pretty badass, a flannel tied around her waist, with holey black stockings. She bumps my hip.

"How's the grades, Lover?" she asks, telling me with her eyes that she's shat the bed as well.

"I didn't even look."

She points. "Whoa, is that your mom's diary?"

I nod and pass it over. She flips through.

"I only read the first entry," I say, feeling weird to have it out of my hands. "Like, I only have it in me to read one at a time."

"What did you learn so far?" Caden asks. I assume Frankie told him about it. Usually, that was how things worked in our posse, Frankie the nucleus.

"Back in 1996, my mom tried to convince my dad to go with Courtney Love's record company."

"STFU," Frankie says.

"Can we get out of here?" I ask, my brow lined with sweat. "These walls, these people, I'm getting claustrophobic."

We reconvene outside by the track where the burn-outs smoke cigarettes and vape. It smells like grape throw up, but it's better than the fake travesty that's the school's halls.

"I found out my grandpa has cancer too," I say, sniffling back tears, even though I don't really know him too well. I'm more so crying because I haven't gotten the chance.

Frankie traces circles across my back. "I'm sorry, Love," she says, and I hope she doesn't stop.

"My mom was checking in with him but hasn't in

two months, meaning she could be anywhere."

"What if you tried to find her?" Caden asks.

Frankie and I are both startled by this, since Caden not only doesn't speak much, but rarely offers a wild idea. He once said he's literally at his happiest doing nothing, just sitting and thinking.

"Where would I start?" I ask, playing along because joking is making me sniffle less.

Franke jumps up and down. "No, Caden's totally right! You could visit everyone from your mom's past, her family and friends, and see if anyone knows more about where she went."

"I don't know most of the people in her life." I shout the rest at the heavens. "I barely know her!"

Frankie hands back the diary, and I clutch it close to my chest. She's excited, I can tell.

"*You* said you never noticed the diary in the attic before. Maybe she left it for you?"

"I had thought that, like a source of clues."

Her nose twitches. "Exactly. Aren't most of her people in L.A.?"

"You mean like a road trip?" I say, as if it's a secret. I knew that my mom had run away after her sister Kristen died. She made a mixtape and traveled up California into Oregon where she met my dad before winding up in Seattle, hoping to meet Kurt Cobain. It's in my blood to follow that reckless abandon. I could start with my grandparents in L.A., especially Grandpa Peter to make sure he's doing okay, even go visit Great Aunt Carly up in Ojai too.

"You think your dad would let you?" Caden asks, the sensible one.

"Probably, I'd bill it as staying with family." A lightbulb goes off. "And then, I could see my mom's friends from high school. She had a trio, kinda like we do. This girl Winter, I mean, she's a woman now. I think she has her own daughter. And her friend Jeremy, who I believe runs a hair salon by the beach."

Frankie claps. "This is settled, we're going."

Caden's eyes bug, but he nods in agreement.

"You guys want to come too?" I ask, dumbfounded.

"Of course. We can't let you go alone," Frankie says. "Besides, what were we doing this summer anyway? Listening to all the alterna tracks of 1997? We can make our own mixtape to go with the trip. I know!" She gets out her Walkman and pops it open. The Red Hot Chili Peppers, "Californication". She closes it and pushes play until we can hear Anthony Kiedis crooning through the headphones. "'Californication', we can start with that song!"

And now, I'm not sad anymore, I'm psyched. The three of us sway to the Chili Peppers. I feel closer to my mom than I have been in a while. She's hovering, pulsing, calling me to her. We'll search in every nook in L.A., through her past until her secrets are revealed. This is what she wanted. This will bring us close together.

"Like, you're serious right?" I ask. "Will your parents let you go?"

Frankie's eyebrows turn to lightning bolts. "I mean, I know my mom won't care. And she's been doing better. She hasn't gone on her night walks in some time. Her medication just needed to be shifted."

We both turn to Caden, knowing his moms tend

to be the strictest. One is a lawyer and always wears pantsuits, the other a nurse. They have a chart in the kitchen outlining each of their chores. I think the lawyer mom makes them.

Caden shrugs. "They'll probably be glad I won't be sitting around at home."

Frankie taps her chin. "This is how we bill it: a cultural exploration of Los Angeles. Take in the art museums. And we'll have supervision the entire time with your grandparents."

"I'm sure they'll be happy to have me...us."

"And your dad can't say no to that," Frankie adds. "I know! You say you want to be there for them during this difficult time while your mom has gone. And it'd be easier with us around too."

"Yeah, he would go for that."

"It's settled then," Frankie says, putting her hand out palm down. I place mine on top and Caden does the same.

"9021-*Hole*!" we chant, getting glares from the burnouts.

"What?" Frankie snaps. "Get out of your weed clouds for one moment of your lives, we're headed to L.A." She sings off-key. "Cali-for-ni-cation."

I picture us with the wind in our hair driving down the PCH on our mission. Maybe my mom ran away again because she knew I needed something to wake me up, get me pumped, less of a blob. She vanished to give my life purpose in finding her again.

Frankie danced to the Chili Peppers in her head, dipping and weaving, pawing at her thick, messy hair, beckoning me to join as I fell in her arms and did a jig, not caring that someone murmured "Ghosts" under their breath. We were weird and I wouldn't have it any other way. No one else had friends like I did, friends who truly cared. Caden leaped into our jubilation, bopping his head to the soft beat still coming from the headphones. We were the only three people on Earth at that moment, and I cried, a little for my mom, but more because I was surrounded in our little bubble with so much true love. We find our own families, even when ours are broken.

I brush by Frankie and my lips graze her cheek. She smells like delicious soap. I take a whiff, hold it in my nostrils, as she tilts her arms to the sky, her eyes closed and kissed by the sun, her dance never-ending and always beautiful.

I reach for the sky too, tug on a passing cloud.

7

· · · · ·

YOU WERE MEANT FOR ME – JEWEL

May 20, 1997

We go on tour for Evanico's first album, *Dreams Are a Design,* which the critics have embraced, calling it a "Quiet reflection on themes of love and coming-of-age," and "A tour de force of post-post-grunge sound." Others said, "Nico Sullivan is a powerful chanteuse that rivals Stevie Nicks [and] Evan Marvin channels great guitarists from long past effortlessly." We do a Lilith Fair concert with Fiona Apple, Joan Osborne, Tracy Chapman, and Paula Cole, our favorite moment—a stripped-down duet of Jewel's "You Were Meant for Me", with the coolest multi-million-selling gal from Alaska who rides horses and can lasso. Instead of a raging mosh-pit, young girls in long, muddy dresses sway with lighters. I retire my Doc Martins and flannels and pick up purple-tinted sunglasses, copy their floral hippie dresses, grow my hair long with blonde highlights and henna tattoos on my hands, Birkenstocks for my callused feet. Evan doesn't change at all, still in his moldy green sweater, something I respect, quietly strumming at the back of the stage with no interest in pushing to the front.

Turns out Courtney Love's record company wasn't in line with our sound, still firmly signing rock bands. But when Astral heard of their interest in us, they jumped. Gave us full control in what we wanted for the album without much pushback. And recording was a dream (hence the name of the record), just Evan, Dave Grohl the cat and I creating art, cracking open our minds, and eager for whatever spilled out. The album came fast and neither of us touched alcohol or pot during the sessions. I didn't crave it like I used to, content with Evan.

Lilith Fair led to a full tour across the states and Europe. Our singles were staying on the charts, the music videos firmly in the top ten on *TRL.* Carson Daly called us a "band to watch," then things started to change. Evan and I were having our ups and downs. We were too busy. Dave Grohl died in a dramatic, terrible way, his final meows piercing my heart. I was dropping too much E. The record company asked about a second album, and then in Amsterdam after a long set, I threw up. The next morning, I threw up again. We cancelled our next show in Ghent and I figured I should go to the doctor. That was when I found out I was pregnant.

I didn't tell Evan right away, not wanting anything to hiccup our plans. The next album—that needed to be the focus. When we returned back to the States, we had literally one day off. That was when I told him.

He was excited. His blue eyes dancing. I hadn't expected that reaction. I thought he would be mad. I don't know, I'd never been pregnant before. I was only nineteen. He spoke about taking the baby on tour, giving it huge headphones so its tiny ears wouldn't be hurt by the loud sounds. He got me hyped up about being a mother.

My family was less enthused. My dad had become our partial manager, since he was in finance already. He saw how much dough was rolling in and knew any time off could kill our career. My mom didn't think I was ready to become a mom, which got us into ongoing argument about her being a good one. I wasn't trying to be mean, only honest. She often liked to say that she "did her best" in terms of raising me and Kristen. She didn't understand that she raised us both very differently, especially after Kristen died and she kinda checked out.

"I don't want to make those same mistakes," I said to her.

Sometimes you can hear yourself saying something, but you don't believe those words actually came from out of your mouth. I'd expressed to my parents about their shortcomings when I ran away from home after Kristen passed. I told them that I wouldn't have needed to run away had they been mentally there for me. We'd gotten to a much better place when Grenade Bouquets went on tour, but this upended any kind of progress. I guess my mom had a lot of truth-bombs she'd been holding onto for a long time. She called me "selfish" and used cliches like "two-way street", trying to make a point that I was as difficult a daughter as she was a mom. She said having a baby so young would "ruin my life" and that Evan and I weren't "even married". I called her "outdated", that I could be a mom and a singer and not have to give either up. Sad thing was it put a wedge between us that seemed to linger. Then she was getting married to her neighbor Roger Ferguson and warned me not to ruin her moment. So, I decided not to go to the wedding, and we haven't spoken since. Dad tried to mediate, but I took his control away as our financial manager, and then he stopped speaking with me too.

We toured a little during the early months of my pregnancy, but then I began to have doubts. There was still time to get an abortion. I waffled between giving it up, but ultimately wanted to have it to show my parents they were wrong. I know, a stupid reason to have a baby, but I can be a stupid girl. Stubborn. Prone to lashing out. Jealous and needy. Great mom material, right?

We told Astral and they supported whatever we decided. They only needed to know one way or the other, so they could cancel the spots on the tour around when I'd be giving birth. They suggested Evan and I take a few days in Big Bear where one of the execs had a weekend house. He wanted us to sit with this life-changing decision and really weigh the pros and cons. So, Evan and I packed up the car and drove to Big Bear. I was three months pregnant, feeling like crap, stuffing my face with every weird food combination I could find, not talking to my parents, and only in touch with my old best friends for advice. Jeremy was busy with starting school at Vidal Sassoon in Santa

Monica, but Winter was around. When we stopped for gas midway, I gave her a ring. It'd been too long since we spoke.

"Hey, Nico Nicotine," she said, in her sing-song tone. She might've been high. I was being good, since I was with child. The worst thing I'd put in my body was sushi despite the doctor's orders about the dangers of raw fish.

I caught her up to speed and she agreed my parents were dicks, always have been. She'd put off college, gotten a job at a CD store in DTLA where she was sleeping with her boss who had the unfortunate name Fang. Typical Winter.

"So, you'll make a choice after this weekend?" she asked.

I pictured her childhood bedroom, still surrounded by music posters. Pearl Jam became Marilyn Manson and now a new idol had overtaken her walls. It made me sad to realize I had no idea who she listened to now.

"What if this is the only time I'll ever get the chance to be a mom?" I asked, twisting the heavy metal phone cord around my finger.

"Okay," she said. "Picture it, you wanna record an album, but you got a loaded diaper to deal with. And not just a normal diaper, this kid shat up a storm and it's *everywhere*. Does that excite you?"

I made a face. "Well, no. Of course not."

"That's your answer then."

"There's more to motherhood than cleaning up shit."

"Not for the first few years," Winter said, as if she

was speaking from wise experience.

"Hey, lemme ask you," I said. "Whose posters do you have up all over your walls now?"

"You're gonna think I'm lame." She let out a breath that I imagined was a weed cloud. "You, Nico. Evanico."

My heart boomed. "Really?"

"Yeah, maybe I've matured too. I like that sweet sound now. No more ripping heads off baby birds. Well, you know what I mean."

I smiled. "I think I do. Love you, Winter."

"And of course, my favorite song is the one about me. 'Winter'. I'm famous."

"You are. And always will be."

"I know, Nic Nic. Good luck up in Big Bear. And whatever you choose, I'm in your corner. Whether it involves loaded diapers or not."

I hung up and got back in the car with Evan. He massaged my shoulder.

"Ready," he said, and I stared at him for a few seconds, enough for it to be uncomfortable.

"I think so," I finally said.

He turned on the radio and "You Were Meant for Me" played as we drove off into the mountains.

Was the baby I carried meant for me?

Jewel, like an oracle, giving me a nudge?

8

• • • • •

NO EXCUSES – ALICE IN CHAINS

I return home, armed and ready with excuses for my L.A. trip, not expecting to find Marjorie there. She has her brown hair up in a bun with a clip to keep it in place, wearing what I like to think of as librarian glasses. She sits with my dad at the kitchen table and they both turn to me as if I might have information about where Mom went. I can see it in his eyes, the hope. I swear I won't let him down. Over speakers, Alice in Chains "No Excuses" softly plays. There's always music playing in our house.

"Oh, Love, Marjorie came over," he says, as if I can't see her there.

Marjorie envelops me with a hug that I didn't ask for, although I'm not mad at. "I'm so sorry about your mom," she says. "She's gonna turn up. That's what I told your dad."

"She's doing this to mess with me," Dad says, under his breath. "She's done it before."

I sit down at the table. "Really?" There's a bowl

with fruit that's started to turn. I choose a banana that seems the ripest.

"She needs to be the center of attention." He backtracks. "I mean, she used to. I don't know what she's like anymore."

I reach over to give him a side-hug because I can relate.

"Anyway," he says, his eyes brightening. "Enough of her for now. How was the last day of school?"

I'm caught off guard, not expecting his mood to change so quickly. But he and my mom certainly had a weird relationship. Love sprinkled with some hate.

"Can we talk?" I ask, and Marjorie's eyes drop to her folded hands. She stands and pushes in her chair, picks up a box.

"I brought sweets," she says, her voice quivering, afraid of my reaction. I always thought I'd been super nice to Marjorie, but maybe I was my typical mopey self. "Baked them this morning. I remember you like the peach danishes."

I do like the peach danishes.

"Thanks, and uh, you don't have to go," I say. Truth is, I'm glad she's here for my dad. It's strange to share his affection with someone else, but necessary. In two years, I'd be off at college and likely wouldn't stick around Eugene to go to U. of Oregon. "I just wanted to ask my dad something."

"What is it, bug?"

I wince. He used to call me that as a child, but now that I'm older it makes me feel like a little kid. Still, it's not the right time now to correct him.

"I thought about what you said about Grandpa

Peter, and I want to visit him. Actually, I was going to ask if Frankie and Caden could come too? I haven't seen him or Grandma Luanne in a while and they must be sad about Mom, and Frankie and Caden really have nothing to do this summer either. I mean, I don't either. Now that I have a car I could drive down to L.A."

He coughs, chokes on what seems to be an air bubble. "You want to drive to L.A.?"

"You've let me go to Portland for the day. It's easier if I go with a car, so no one would have to drive me around everywhere. You know, L.A. is a car culture."

"Yes, Love, I know L.A," he says, and Marjorie takes his hand and gives it a squeeze. She gives me a look that tells me we're in this together. I instantly like her even more. "How long would you go for?"

"I don't know," I say, going through my mind all the people from mom's past I wanted to see. "Maybe a week, two weeks. I could split my time at both grandparent's houses and even Great Aunt Carly."

"You want to go up to Ojai?" he asks, flabbergasted, like that's the craziest thing.

"Yeah, it would be on the way back anyway. She's always said her door is open whenever I wanted."

"That's true."

"So, you'll let me go?"

He rubs his forehead that has more worry lines than it used to. He's gonna be forty soon, which seems so old, halfway to death. I wonder if that was why my mom took off? A journey to escape middle age.

"Have you even asked Grandpa Peter or Grandma Luanne?"

"I haven't yet, but they're not gonna say no. They

want to see me more. Like, I feel bad it's taken me this long to visit after the last time. And with Mom…"

His lips twist as if he's received a sudden jolt of pain.

"This could help distract me," I continue. "And Frankie and Caden are there for support."

"Have their parents okayed it?" he asks.

"You know Frankie's mom," I say.

"No, I really don't. I think I've met her twice."

"Why don't we call my grandparents first and set that up and then you can talk to Frankie and Caden's folks?"

"Love, you're sixteen," he says, as if I don't already know.

"At sixteen, you must have traveled away from home," I counter back.

"I was in Idaho, there was nowhere to go."

"Evan," Marjorie says, and gives me a wink. "She'll be visiting family. It's really just the drive down. Love, I assume you're a careful driver?"

"Oh, yeah, I am. I had a great teacher." I nod toward Dad.

"I remember," she says, tapping her chin, "when I was sixteen, a few friends and I drove to Seattle to see Nirvana. My parents didn't want me spending the night at a hotel, so we drove back after the show. Got home around three in the morning. And I just couldn't fall asleep. The energy of the crowd, I kept replaying it over and over in my head. Surely, you did something similar, Evan."

"Yeah, what about the Dead Skies; didn't you play shows?" I ask.

"I mean, around Idaho, yeah. But my parents were

different. My brother had gone off to Iraq—they weren't really thinking about me. Their eyes were glued to the news."

"Dad, you know that I don't touch alcohol or drugs, like no. So what trouble could we get into? It's only the long drive to L.A. and we'll stop only to use the bathroom and get food. We'll leave first thing in the morning and get there by late night."

"It's like a thirteen-hour drive," Dad says, the tone of his voice telling me he was having second thoughts. He probably had been leaning toward it until he calculated the time.

"The three of us will switch off. Frankie and Caden have their licenses now too. Like, we're all really good drivers. And coming back, we'll break up the trip with Carly. Look, if you want, we'll do that both ways and spend the night with her. Then it's only about nine or ten hours. Is that better?"

"Yeah, that would be better," he says, and now I can tell I'm wearing him down.

"So, three hours and change for each of us, that's nothing. And it'll be good practice behind a wheel! There's really *no excuses* you can have."

I give a nod to the Alice in Chains song about to end. He gives a gruff laugh.

"Okay, okay, Love, you convinced me. *But...* everyone else still has to agree."

"They will, they will."

I tackle him with a hug and kiss him on his scruffy cheek. He's smiling a little now, which is better than when I first walked in. Marjorie seems downright giddy too.

"I'll make dinner tonight," I declare. "You both put your feet up and relax."

I shoo them over to the TV couch.

"Okay, okay," Dad repeats, sitting down with Marjorie and putting his arm around her. It shocks me at first, seeing them like a true couple. I have to take a breath. She snuggles against him and I back away.

"I'll call the grandparents and then start on the food. How about zucchini lasagna? I can whip that up fast."

I head back to the kitchen, eyeing them together. I know my mom is still missing and both of us hurt because of that, but like, it doesn't have to rule our emotions all the time. It's not fair for her to hold that kind of power. I hate to say it but she doesn't deserve it. She may have vanished now on a grand scale, but she's been vanishing throughout my whole life, spending more time away than getting to know me. This thought shocks me, the cruelty my mind can go to. I want to find her, *absolutely*, but if she's not interested in being found, I understand that there's nothing I can do. This is a last-ditch effort. And whatever the outcome, I had to except it, even if that means our story has ended.

I hope that Marjorie is more than just a Band-Aid for my dad, and he can feel the same—whatever the outcome of my search may be.

9

· · · · ·

I THINK THAT I WOULD DIE – HOLE

October 24, 1997

Love is due in a week. Yes, that's what we decided to call her, obviously after Courtney the Great. Evan canceled all our tour dates so I could focus on having the baby. He thought there would be too much temptation on the road, which pissed me off. Like, does he not think I'm capable enough of forgoing any substances while a child is inside of me? I would never do anything to endanger Love.

After we came back from a really positive trip to Big Bear, we decided under no circumstance to get an abortion. I was already leaning this way, but he made it clear. Evan wanted a family with me and now Love. He knew it would make things difficult for Evanico, but he didn't care. We were his first priority and always will be.

I admit, it was sweet to hear that. To know he cared that much. Now that I was in the public eye, I was used to people wanting things from me. Unsure if someone liked me for me, or my stage presence. But not Evan. He knew me before I was famous, unlike anyone else new in my life. And therefore, he could be trusted. But I can never let things be. I always have to stir up drama. It's like drama finds me no matter where I go. So, I found myself lashing out at him. On the outside looking in, he was being great. The supportive boyfriend who actually began talking about marriage. But he was becoming my keeper. Checking up on me like he didn't trust me to make good decisions. I, for one, would *not* have cancelled our tour dates until I was about to burst. Astral supported this decision, but it was a bad move. Here we had built-up momentum and then we vanish. Fans are fickle and they would move on. There was a glut of similar bands in the spotlight now and we'd fade into the darkness. I could see it and it frightened me.

I was also struggling with the idea of being a mom, but not letting that define me. To make up for my own mom's mistakes (who I still wasn't speaking to), I'd try to be the best mom I could be, but not at the detriment (SAT word!) to my career. So, my timebomb self-made this all clear to Evan.

"I feel like a slug," I said, one blustery day in October. Love was on her way and even the excitement of this new tiny being couldn't shift my mood. I was realizing that more and more. I'd get in moods and they'd sink my whole day. Sometimes over the littlest thing. Evan was kinda the opposite and that annoyed me too. It's not like he was the most upbeat person out there, but he always had a positive outlook, where

I enjoyed stewing.

We started doing this awkward dance where he was afraid of saying anything that could set me off, and I'd go nuts to compensate for having *nada* to argue about. Healthy right? Not so much.

Like one day, he was fixing a shelf that had fallen. A few books slid to the floor. *Going Down* by Jennifer Belle, which I had devoured. *Prozac Nation*, not the best for my headspace. He had nails in his mouth. "You should be resting now."

Tick. Tick. Tick.

"Why should I be resting?" I shouted. "What are you trying to say about women, that we're weak? That my frail body requires constant feet up or I'll melt?"

I was heaving, holding my belly, foaming at the mouth. He backed up, his hands in the air. Tossed the long hair out of his eyes.

"Whoa, I didn't mean anything like that."

"You made the decision to cancel the tour without even running it by me."

"It's not healthy for you. It's exhausting doing shows even when you're not pregnant—"

"I hate this bullshit *feeble* label you've put on me. This delicate thing that might shatter at any second."

"I don't think I've ever said that."

"Fine, I made it up because evidently I'm a liar and hysterical too."

He left the room. That's how he'd usually end arguments—by walking away. Maybe I knew this and that's why I pushed. Hoping once that he'd fight back. It was one thing to care about me, and he did, I knew that. But it's another to really fight for me, for us. And he never did. He hated conflict and would slink away. So that's how I began seeing him, as an abandoner.

It got really lonely. I didn't have Evan to talk to, or my parents, and Winter and Jeremy seemed like they'd moved on from having me around. Winter was living with this guy Fang, who she worked with at the CD store. Fang was older, which wasn't a surprise with Winter, at least she was legal now, but he was Bad News Bears. Not on the level of her last boyfriend, but Fang sold weed as a side business, and it sounded like he was cheating on her (her mom Edina put that bug in my ear). But what I've learned with Winter is you could *never* tell her what to do. If she made mistakes, she needed to make them on her own. She had firmly decided against college (not like I hadn't done the same), but what I couldn't let go was that she rarely wanted to hear about the problems with me and Evan, or about Love. So, I stopped really checking in so much.

With Jeremy, he was so busy at Vidal Sassoon that he never had time, and he'd gotten his first real boyfriend, Lo. Lo lived in Venice and owned a clothing boutique on Melrose called JAZZ and Jeremy would regale me with stories of parties up and down the shores of L.A. and all the famous people he'd see, like Ian Ziering surfing one day. I wanted to talk about all the famous people in my orbit (hello, Jewel!), but that seemed like showing off, so I kept mum. Jeremy had spent most of our friendship listening to everything going on in mine and Winter's life, so it was my turn to do the same. Still, it seemed like whenever I called, he picked up out of breath and was always running somewhere, so eventually I stopped calling too.

All the new famous folks I'd met as well were people I'd call friends, but not the kind of friends you'd share your darkest secrets with. Jewel was lovely, Sarah McLachlan was amazing, Joan Osborne badass, Natalie Merchant, my sister from another mother, but they were all so much older than I was, and even though I was pregnant and moving away from being a teen, I still felt like a baby compared to them, unworthy of their time.

So, it was a lot of chilling with soon-to-be Love. Rubbing my stomach and imagining who'd she become. Would she be the first woman president, or a kick ass rocker like me? Would she be kind, or difficult, funny or serious? It freaked me out to think I'd have to love this creature unconditionally, even if she was a demon spawn.

The only person in my life who'd make sure to check in and see how I was doing was Aunt Carly.

"Sweetness," she'd say, when she'd call. She wouldn't monopolize the conversation with everything going on in her life. Usually it was an art show, some drama with her cats, or maybe a new gentleman suitor. She'd mostly listen and that was gold for me. I'd tell her about my depression, my moods, my hesitancy about being a mom for the rest of my existence, the difficulties Evan and I were having, and she'd never judge.

"But what should I do?" I asked, wanting this soothsayer to solve all of my ills.

"You can only be the best Nico you can be every day. For Evan, for your fans, for this new Love that you're bringing into the world, but most of all for yourself. If you can't love yourself, how can you love anyone else?"

I was listening to "I Think That I Would Die" by Hole. *I want my baby, where is my baby, I want my baby.* I felt if I played Courtney Love's music to Love in the womb some of it might seep into my uterus.

"I hate myself sometimes," I said, biting my lip. I had never outwardly admitted that before, but it was true. My body could be a slog to exist in, for everyone around me, but most of all, for myself.

"Nico," she said. "Everyone has hated themselves at one point. We all are a product of our mistakes. The secret is finding whatever way you can *to* love yourself, even if it's rough some days and you feel like giving up. This might not come easy for you. You may have to really search for it, so spend your life searching, find what makes you love yourself whether it's music, or Evan, this new Love coming into the world, or something else entirely."

"What is it for you?" I asked, breathless, as if she held the entire secret of the universe in her watercolor-stained fingers.

"Not for me to really say, because for you it won't be the same. Sometimes it's painting, sometimes my kitties, sometimes even the bond you and I have. It can be many things. But I'm still seeking too, that's the key. Always expanding my core, my aura."

"Hmmm, I think I get it."

"You're about to have to become selfless. Because your child will need that care. But your child won't be cared for properly unless you care well enough for yourself. You see? It's more important now than ever. And always will be."

I thought about these wise words, long after our conversation ended, and I sat up in the middle of night because I couldn't get comfortable enough sleeping. I stared out of my rain-streaked window and wondered if I'd already encountered this special thing, which would make me whole. Could it be waiting for me in a week when Love would be born, or was it many years away, hidden far from where I thought I should look, and one day I'd find the courage in me to go, to be happy, to chase this shine?

And with that, my water broke.

10

. . . . .

Turns out the drive to Ojai from Eugene clocks in at about thirteen hours. Frankie, Caden, and I split it up three ways like we promised my dad we would. My grandparents were both overjoyed to have us. Well, Grandpa Peter doesn't seem the type of be overjoyed about anything, but he still seemed touched that I wanted to spend time with him. His wife Annette owned a French restaurant in Los Feliz called *Tartuffe* and was jazzed to try out some specials on us. Grandma Luanne gushed about all the things we'd do: a Dodgers game, the Getty Museum, but I told her we really only wanted to hang around the house with her and Mr. Ferguson. I was here to glean info about my mom, not have a vacation.

Frankie's spacey mom agreed without much resistance, but Caden's moms took a bit more convincing. Both grandparents had to call them and assure that their child would be well looked after. Caden had never even been to sleepaway camp before, so this was the longest he and his moms would ever be apart. I think when they realized that, they changed their minds and figured it was time to cut the cord.

We had my dad's credit card for an emergency, and I gave him a tearful hug when we left. I had spent time away from him before: camp and a trip once to Turino with my school, but this would be the first time I was really on my own, at least for the drive there. I promised I'd be super cautious and call him when we arrived in Ojai no matter what time. And so, we were off!

I had a bunch of mixtapes for the ride and had made a new one that added some of the songs on our 1997ish list along with cuts my mom mentioned in her diary. It was weird to read the parts about myself. To hear her hesitation about having me. But more than that, she offered her first clue about where she might be. She was searching for a way to love herself. Obviously, she'd reached a point in her life where her music career *and me* were not enough. So, I was less worried that she might be hurt out there. She was finding herself right now, the question being—where?

We reach Ojai at around eight at night, wiped from driving since six in the morning, "Beautiful Disaster" by 311 the last song we shut off midway. But we're buzzed as we hop out of the car. The air is cool and smells sweet. Wind chimes dance on Carly's door, as she opens it upon our arrival. Two black and white cats chase each other through her legs and dart past us. I pick up one and give it a kiss before it wiggles out of my grasp. Carly's wearing a shawl and hot pants, the shawl hanging off one shoulder like she's in an eighties' aerobics video, her hair fully gray now, long down her back, a statement necklace with a pink crystal reflecting from the moonlight.

"Love," she says, extending her arms and beckoning me to come. I fold into her bones like a baby bird, tears falling. I sniff them away. Somehow, I feel closer to my mom when hugging Carly and I don't want to let go. "Come in, come in."

Inside, the pink crystal around her neck is duplicated in art pieces around her house. More cats slink around and a record plays Janis Joplin. She has no lights on, only candles flickering, the large windows wide open, Ojai pouring in. I introduce Frankie and Caden and we reconvene at the dining table. She's made us tofu dishes, soaked in mirin with an heirloom tomato salad. The three of us are starving and scarf it down. Then she opens a bottle of wine and asks if we want any. None of us are drinkers so we decline. She has lemonade instead and we have them in decal glasses in her living area, surrounded by more cats that seem to pop up out of nowhere.

"Well, Love," she says, her teeth already stained red. Janis Joplin has been replaced with Crosby, Stills and Nash. "You've grown so. You're developing."

I look down at my chest, thinking she means my breasts, but she shakes her head.

"No, your energy, that's what's matured. You've shed your childhood."

"Your place is so cool," Frankie says, flipping through records positioned on the mantel above her fireplace.

"Thank you," Carly says, her eyes sparkling. "It's

been my home most of my life, pretty much since I was your age. Well, Ojai at least." She takes my hand, her mouth turning to a frown. "I'm so sorry, Love. I haven't heard from your mother. But I'm sure she's okay."

I'm not ready for this turn in the conversation. We had kept it light at dinner. Carly asked about our interests, school, who we had crushes on (even though that's not a light subject!).

I pick at a thread on her couch. One of her cats gives me a look to stop, so I do.

"Yeah, that's really the point of this trip," I say, and Frankie and Caden nod. "Talk to people from her past, see if anyone might have any ideas about where she went."

Carly lights a candle in front of her that smells of lilac, illuminating her face.

"I can't say I'll be much help with that. I don't know a lot of the people in your mom's orbit. We have a very isolated relationship the two of us."

"But isn't it weird that she hasn't called you?"

Carly thinks on this. "Not quite, sometimes we go a few months without speaking. I will say this about Nico, I tend to be able to sense when she's about to reach out. It's a sixth sense I have."

And quietly, I ask: "You don't feel that now?"

"No, but that doesn't mean tomorrow will be different." She takes a gulp of wine, the bottle now a third finished. "People require so much from each other sometimes. Always interacting. At least your generation."

"Not me," I say, showing her my flip phone. "Or

Frankie or Caden, none of us have smart phones, we're not on social media."

"So, you should understand the need for someone to unplug, Love."

"Do you think that's all my mom is doing? Unplugging?"

"It might not be our business what she's doing."

But I'm her daughter, I want to yell. Everything she does should be my business.

Frankie clears her throat. "I think Love is just worried. Like, it's fine for her mom to want some time to herself, but she should've given a heads-up."

Carly turns to Frankie, takes her in. "Do you always speak for Love?" she asks.

Frankie and I look at each other screwy.

"What do you mean?" I ask, as Carly stands and dances toward the record player, lowering the volume.

"An interesting trio you three," she says, with a bit of a sway. I wonder how much she's affected by the wine.

My body throbs, not liking where this is going. "What do you mean by that?"

"Trios in general. The power dynamics. One is always left out."

She eyes Caden as if he's the obvious one.

"Do you speak?" she asks him, raising her eyebrows.

"Caden's shy," Frankie adds.

"You like speaking for others, don't you?"

Carly returns to her bottle, pours another glass.

Frankie crosses her arms. "I think you've had enough."

Carly chuckles. "Oh, I'm messing with you all. Let

an old woman have her fun. I was trying to change the mood."

"By insulting us?" Frankie says, arms still crossed.

"By challenging you. Your dynamics have always been the same, I presume, because they haven't been challenged. You see each other at school, at each other's homes after school, the weekends, but it's all centered around your lives in Eugene. Now here, you're on a road trip. Your first as your father has explained to me. And trust this old woman, will you? Things will change between the three of you on this trip."

Caden gulps audibly.

"Now it may be for the better, and it may be for the worse. What you can't understand as teens yet is that not all relationships stay the same for the rest of your life. We morph, we mutate, we require different things from one another. As you all will do. Maybe as friends? Maybe as more?"

I'm watching Frankie the whole time. She has her eyes fixed on Carly, but I have no idea the thoughts running through her skull. I only know my own. And that those are very confused. I love Frankie, that's obvious. Everyone who's ever encountered Frankie and has half a brain has loved her. But maybe I *love*, love her more than a friend. The past year, these thoughts have crept more and more into my cranium. The desire to want to be around her all the time. The way we can be with each other for hours and it feels like no time has passed. I've never had these feelings about someone else. But then, the thought of kissing her like that guy with the long darting tongue did to me? I'm not sure I want that. I don't know if I think of her in *that* way. So, hence the confusion. And it's heightened even more because I've had the sneaking sense that Caden pines for her in the same way. Frankie, once again, the nucleus.

"I'm tired," Carly declares, the back of her hand covering her yawn. "Come nine o'clock I'm usually long in bed. It's the mornings where I thrive. Each couch turns into a bed, and I have a sleeping bag for the floor."

She scoops up the bottle and whisks by me on her way to the bedroom.

"Wake up early, Love. Just you and me, we'll watch the sun."

"Okay," I say, and she leaves a wet kiss on my cheek.

We set up our beds and lie down, blowing out a few of the candles, the lights so dim we can pretty much only see each other's eyes. The Crosby, Stills and Nash record nears its end leaving the sound of the speakers static. None of us know what to say. It's been a long day, and my eyes are super tired, but I can't go to bed without mentioning what Carly said about 9021-*Hole*. How obvious it was that both Caden and I orbited around Frankie.

"Your great aunt certainly likes her wine," Frankie says, crossing her eyes like she's drunk. Caden laughs and Frankie throws a couch pillow at him.

"I'm sorry?" I say, more like a question, since I'm unsure I'm actually sorry. This is my chance to get into Frankie's head, tool around. "But she's right, ya-know?"

Frankie narrows her eyes. "How is she right?"

"You are the nucleus." I look over at Caden to verify, but he's focusing on the pillow in his lap.

"That's ridiculous—"

"Caden, have you or I *ever* hung out just the two of us?" I ask. It comes off snotty, but I don't mean it to be.

"Uhhh, I dunno."

That's all I'd get from Caden. Truth being we haven't. We all met the first week as freshman. Everyone cliquing up so fast we were left spinning like three lonely tops. Caden and I were sitting alone in the cafeteria on opposite ends of a table. Frankie came over and sat down directly in the center, started talking about nothing and everything. She talked so fast it was like a tennis match keeping up with what she said. Caden and I were both in awe.

"So what?" she says, flinging her blanket off. "I'm the nucleus. What does that even mean and who cares? I'm the loudest of all of us, so it's natural that I'm the center. It doesn't mean that I have more power or whatever than the two of you."

My voice is small, a tiny mouse when I say, "I think we idolize you."

Frankie does a spit take, even though she doesn't have anything in her mouth.

Caden puts the pillow over his face.

I'm singing the song "Beautiful Disaster" in my head and thinking about what a disaster this night has become.

"Idolize me? Stupid me? Like why?"

And behind his pillow, Caden murmurs: "You say the things we want to say but can't." He lowers the pillow, looking so fragile. "Like, I get so nervous talking…to *anyone*. Sometimes I wish I was you, Frankie."

"Okay, I'm not seeing how this is a bad thing," Frankie says.

"It's not!" I chirp. "Carly didn't say it was bad. She was simply pointing out our dynamics."

"What gives her the right?"

"Maybe we needed an outsider perspective," I say. "We're so exclusive, like we never let anyone else in."

"So, you want other friends, Love, is that what you're saying?"

"No, *never*, maybe just for you to be more aware."

I don't even know what I'm babbling, my words independent from my brain.

Frankie cocks her head. "Aware of what?"

"How we…" I catch Caden's eye, and he holds it this time. "How we feel about you."

The room gets quiet, a cat meows, the lights dimmer than before. Frankie has to know what I'm hinting at, but maybe it makes her uncomfortable, so she doesn't bite.

"I need to go to bed," she declares. "You two hens can stay up yapping all night, but I'm done."

And with that, she puts in earplugs and disappears under her blanket. Caden and I still watch one another, both goading for the other to pony up our true feelings first. He shrugs and gets under the covers as well.

I sigh and blow out the candles, but I'd be a fool to think I could sleep at all.

• • •

Before sunrise, Carly wakes me with her coffee breath at my ear. Frankie and Caden are lumps under their blankets. I'm groggy as she leads me outside, places a peppermint tea in my hands that smells so good.

"Not good to get into a caffeine habit so young," she whispers. "You'll never kick it."

We sit on her front porch, the wind chimes dancing, as the sun begins red and warm at the bottom of the mountains. I lean on her shoulder.

"She feels so far away," I say. I could feel Carly nod.

She touches my heart. "She's never far away if she's always here."

"I have her diary with me."

I look up and can see Carly's eyebrows have raised.

"What does it say?"

"I can only read one entry at a time," I say, telling myself this over and over again, maybe because I'm afraid of seeing my mom unravel more and more. "I found it in the attic, but it never was there before. At least, I'm not sure. Do you think she left it for me?"

A tabby cat slinks by and Carly places it in her lap.

"This is Beau. He's a scamp. Sometimes he leaves me dead mice at the foot of my bed. It's garbage, but he thinks it's a gift."

"So, the diary might be garbage?"

She shakes her head. "I'm saying it might mean something entirely different to you and your mom."

I'm whispering, "I think she left it for me."

"Then you believe that, child. I'm not gonna tell you otherwise."

The sun turns orange as it looks like it's being pulled by a string into the sky. Its heat infectious.

"You tell my brother Peter hi for me when you see him. I may not like him most of the time, but I love him."

"I will."

"And go to L.A. as an adventure, not a treasure hunt. The Tohono O'odham tribe believes in the man in the maze. Life in a nutshell. With each twist and turn, we become stronger as a person. The journey, not the destination."

I take in her advice. I'd been telling myself that I couldn't be upset if I don't find the answers I seek, but that's a lie. What I need out of this trip may be impossible in the end.

Carly kisses the top of my head and stands.

"I'll make you and your friends some egg sammies for the road. I think you've gotten what you've needed here."

I'm about to say something in response, but she walks back into the house. The tabby cat left behind, staring through my soul. Telling me that I'd been given words of wisdom and I should be lucky. And if I don't take that advice, it's my fault for having too great expectations.

The cat blinks and darts back into the house too.

I can already smell the eggs being fried in grease.

11

• • • • •

FELL ON BLACK DAYS – SOUNDGARDEN

January 3rd, 1998

I feel like I'm in a fog. I'm not sleeping. Love is a colicky baby and a lingering dread courses through my body. I have to wake up multiple times in the night to feed her and then I can't get back to sleep, or nap during the day. When the sun sets, I get anxious at the night ahead, the long hours. Evan can see the thick purple sacks under my eyes. He offers to stay up with Love, but I know that won't work. It's my breast or nothing. Being the most important person in her life comes with a price. I'm weepy and irritable and at my best when I'm curled up in front of the TV assaulted by images. I watch the Home Shopping Network so much that I get to know the hosts. I call in and order the most ridiculous things. Packages arrive every day and I don't remember using my credit card to pay. I see a doctor who tells me that "all mothers experience this". I want to mention some of my issues, that I'm prone to feeling depressed. That ever since my sister Kristen died, I haven't been whole. That I probably need medication.

But I don't. I stay silent. The doctor labels me overtired and I'm sent home. There Evan is cooing over Love like she's the greatest thing ever created, but I just don't feel that. I look at her and all I see is what she wants from me. My love. My milk. My time. And it seems like she gives nothing in return. Evan suggests music as if it could be our salvation. "Sing to her," he says, and he goes through all the baby songs ad nauseum. Of course, when he pays attention to Love, she's quiet and alert, not even close to tears. When I come by, her monster switch turns on. She observes me as if she doesn't trust me at all, and I can understand. I'm unworthy of being a mama and should've listened to my parents and aborted her when I had the chance.

I'm aware that if anyone saw what I've written they'd be horrified. On stage, I'm a goddess with my long hair in curls, barefoot in the mud with a tambourine, but in reality, I'm absolute filth. Sometimes I wish for them all to know my true self so I don't have to pretend anymore. To the fans, to Evan. I think he's starting to suspect.

We should be creating our next album, but the thought of putting pen to paper, or even for a song to expel from my throat, seems impossible. I can sit in the attic away from Love's cries and play Soundgarden's "Fell on Black Days" over and over, and that's it. I can become one with that song, as if Chris Cornell has created it just for me. He would understand my plight. No one else.

I've taken to sneaking nips of alcohol. I believe Evan has begun to monitor, knowing I'm still breast feeding, so I drink only the clear liquids and replace it with water. I do it mostly in the middle of the night when I should be feeding her—seeing her cry out, numb to her distress. Only when I'm wobbling can I pick her up and coo. Whether because of this, or because he sees me disintegrating, Evan suggests moving Love to formula, so I can sleep at night. We do this for a week, and I spend that week only sleeping, stopping to use the bathroom and occasionally put food in my system. After that week, nothing was the same.

Evan and Love had bonded in my absence more than they ever had before. He became protective over her, fearing her safety if I'd try to take control. He was probably right, since I spent most the day as a disposal for alcohol. He tried to get me to stop, but I was too wasted to hear. The house started to feel claustrophobic, the walls out to get me. Sleepy Eugene with its rainy winters. I stopped going outside. I lived in the same clothes. I saw the doctor again but still didn't tell him my true problems. I figured he couldn't understand, and no one would help me.

And then a light arrived. Small at first, just a tiny spark. I thought about leaving this newfound family. Taking off—where I did not know, but that grain started to carry me through the days. It wouldn't be forever. Only to hear myself think. I wanted to write songs in empty fields with only the birds as company.

I wanted to see the world beyond Oregon again. I'd gotten a tease of Europe during a too-short tour. I could go back and sit outside of cafes with a journal and a purpose again.

I'd watch them at night, Evan rocking Love, and think of how much better off they'd be without me. I've weighed them down. I could see it in Evan. He was exhausted, not from being a new parent, but from me. Cleaning up my empties. Anticipating my dark moods. Tiptoeing around anything that might set me off. And he didn't deserve that. He had faults like anyone but was caring and sweet. A zillion other girls would line up to be with him. New mothers for Love. Someone that wouldn't liken her to a beast.

This made me cry. I wondered why I wasn't built like all the rest. Why I couldn't just be happy with the wonderful family I created. I had love, money, fame. If that didn't bring me joy, I was afraid that nothing would.

My parents reached out again and again once we had Love. But I kept them away, not because I didn't want them to have a relationship with their grand-daughter, but because I was scared, they'd see my truth. Even Aunt Carly I shunned. I know Evan kept up a relationship with all of them in secret. I could hear hushed calls when he thought I was asleep. But I would refuse to come to the phone. Same with Winter and Jeremy, I iced them out. Didn't want to be near Jeremy's newfound glee, or Winter's superiority. She'd be so glad not to be the basket case for once, and I couldn't take that kind of smugness. I was an island, and so one day, I picked up my island early,

early in the morning before anyone rose, and left.

I stood outside my home realizing that life could go in two very different directions at this moment. Nothing would ever be the same, even if I returned. But I knew deep down that if I didn't leave, I would die. I'd always been angry at Kurt Cobain for killing himself, what I thought was the easy way out, but now I understood. Everyone else had been taking the easy way out since they didn't carry around pain in their heads like I did. Cobain was giving himself the only kind of love he knew he could, the ability to be free. And while I wasn't ready to stuff my torch for good, I did need to be free, like a bird, so I flew away.

Got in my car and ran just like I'd done when I was sixteen. We're guilty of our histories, repeating the same mistakes over and over. This time I'd run away without a destination, without a purpose, only my heart as a guide. Begging for it to beat again like it used to.

And then maybe I'll return, although I can see myself vanishing for so long that my disappearance becomes my actual life.

Goodbye, Evan. Goodbye, Love.

You both deserved better than me.

12

· · · · ·

LAST GOODBYE – JEFF BUCKLEY

When we stop to eat the egg sammies that Carly made for us, I give Dad a call. I'd texted him when we got in and said I was too tired to talk. He picks up right away, like he's been waiting for my call. This makes me sad. That he's sitting alone rattling in a big house while his daughter is far away, and his one love is even farther. But after reading the depressing entry in Mom's diary and how she abandoned me, I need to hear his voice more than ever.

"Love," he says, and I can picture him beaming. "How's the trip going so far?"

We're at a rest stop in Port Hueneme by the beach, deciding to the take the coastal route. Frankie, Caden and I haven't spoken much since we set out in the morning. Frankie popped in a Jeff Buckley CD and that occupied our time from Ojai.

"It's going," I say.

I hear him talking to someone else.

"Who's that?"

"Oh, oh, that's Marjorie."

I look at my watch. It's just past nine in the morning. Way too early for a visit.

"She kind of…" And then his voice gets real quiet. "She spent the night, Love. I dunno, with you gone and your mother…"

I block my free ear. "You don't need to… I mean, you don't have to explain anything, Dad. I like Marjorie. I do."

"I like her too."

"Okay then. Okay."

Interminable awkward silence.

"I need to ask you something," I say, and he probably figures it's about Marjorie, but… "Did you know Mom had a diary?"

More awkward silence. I picture him hemming and hawing.

"I remember a journal. She had it when we were kids, used to carry it around everywhere. On the cover she drew a picture of these two faces almost kissing."

"Yeah, that's the one."

"I haven't seen it in years."

"Well, I found it. In the attic. And I'm reading it."

I'm not sure how he's gonna respond. If he'll get mad. There's nothing I can do about that now over a thousand miles away.

"She never read me any of it."

He says this sadly, his words wading through puddles. I imagine tears building at the corners of his eyes.

"It's really…" I struggle thinking for the right way to explain. "There's some parts that are really hard to read. Like when she had me."

"She was…in a mad state at that time. Love, I don't know how healthy it is for you to have that."

"It sounds like she had postpartum."

"What?"

"Postpartum. We learned about it in health class this year. A lot of women experience it after childbirth, but it seems like she wasn't diagnosed. She spoke of a doctor who shrugged her off. Like, maybe back then it wasn't as obvious when women came in with symptoms. The point is she was powerless."

He lets out a sigh that drags.

"Love, she left you with me when you were a baby. And she didn't come back. Not for a long time. I had no idea where she was, I was raising a kid all on my own. We had to pick up and move in with my parents in Idaho. That was a nightmare. You know your uncle, they were dealing with that, and then all of us in a small house. I mean that was a disaster. And then she doesn't come back until you're like, a year old."

"But she was clinically depressed!"

I'm getting angry now. I don't want to hear anything negative about her, as if she needed someone to have her back. After only a few short entries I feel like I know her more than I ever have.

"I'm not saying she wasn't… Look, I know your mom has dealt with depression for a lot of her life. When we were in the band, I thought I saw it, but we were so young, I didn't understand how to deal with it."

"But did she ever get help?"

I'm crying now, I can hear my voice cracking.

"Of course, in a lot of ways throughout the years.

Therapists, medications, she's had stays before..."

"What does that mean?"

"Places that can help her. Your grandparents would know more, this was long after she and I broke up. I really don't know the specifics."

"But what if it was caught earlier? Like, right after she had me?"

I want him to tell me that she had a chance, that *we* had a chance as a family.

"I'm not sure what it would've done. I think your mom, she...some people are just sicker than others. Sometimes it's physical and other times..."

"Dad, stop talking to me like I'm a child. I'm not a child anymore."

"No, no you're not. You're right. I think...I think your mom really tried, and if I was angry at her before, I'm trying to reconcile that anger. I know if she could have stayed with us, she would've."

The flip-phone is shaking in my hand. I want to flip it away.

"Talk to your grandparents, Love. They'll answer any questions you have. I'll only be guessing if I tell you what I know."

"Okay."

I say it barely more than a peep.

"Now listen," he says. "This is your summer break, okay? I want you to have a great time in L.A. with your friends. Your mom is gonna be all right."

"How do you know?"

"Because she's kind of indestructible. She always comes back, right? Sometimes it just takes her a little longer. So, that's what this is. A little longer."

"A little longer," I repeat.

"Don't go digging around in that journal. It's only gonna make you feel worse."

I'm clutching it now, so tight that my sweaty hand is causing the marker on the front to smudge.

I hear a honk. I look over and Frankie is leaning on the car horn, the door wide open, Jeff Buckley's "The Last Goodbye" slinking through the beach air.

"I gotta go," I say.

"I love you, honey. Please take care."

"Love you too," I say. "Bye."

I hang up and rush over to the car, not wanting to show the distress on my face. Keeping it bottled in for everyone around me but understanding that it will only cause me to explode later on.

I get in the car, and we take off.

13

• • • • •

SHINE – COLLECTIVE SOUL

We stay at Grandma Luanne's place first, the childhood home of my mom in Laurel Canyon. It's a beautiful house that puts mine to shame, archways in every room and a hot tub in the back. Grandpa Roger needs it for his aching sciatica. Grandma Luanne is tinier than I remember, a shriveled version of her former self. A nervous lady with a constant tissue up her sleeve and a leaky nose. Grandpa Roger is the opposite, a large man with a booming presence. He asks us all to pull his finger, his go-to icebreaker.

We stay in my Aunt Kristen's old room, the one who died. Grandma Luanne makes it a point to tell me that they converted it into an office, although I'm not sure what for, since everyone's retired. Grandpa Roger used to have a septic tank business, I think.

She serves us cucumbers with cream cheese on the patio. She asks about my dad. I can tell she's just being nice. I wonder if my mom's parents always thought Dad led her down a bad road, but that couldn't be further from the truth. She asks about Carly too, but I can tell she's being extra nice and really doesn't care.

"Always a free spirit, that one," she says, lips tight in a grimace. "Still with the cats?"

"Yeah, it's a cat party there," I say.

"And you, Love, how's school?"

"School's cool," I say. It's not worth it to let her know about my solid C average.

"And you'll be looking at colleges next year," she says, stirring a tall drink with a metal straw. "Where do you want to go? What do you want to do?"

I blink in response, having no clue about either. Things I like to do: listen to music released before I was born. The end. For all my mom's eccentricities, at least she knew what she wanted to do at my age. And in terms of colleges that would likely accept me, I'm looking at a community college that would accept anyone.

I shrug and pass the baton over to Frankie and Caden, who are fully enjoying their cucumbers with cream cheese. Beg them to give me a reprieve.

"I want to be in fashion," Frankie says, as Grandma Luanne eyes her ensemble. Jeans with a flannel, her thick hair in a side pony. Grandma Luanne smiles thinly.

"And you? Caden?" she asks, clearing her throat.

This is a mystery to me too. Caden, like myself, has really never expressed interest in anything.

"Rock 'N' Roll," he says, hiding behind his bangs.

"*What?*" Frankie and I both ask.

"Yeah, like something with rock 'n' roll," he says. "Maybe a sound engineer?"

This gets a wider smile from Grandma Luanne. "Oooh, sounds interesting."

"The Beatles," Grandpa Roger says. "Now they were a *band*."

We all nod at that.

After our snacks, Grandma Luanne takes me up to my mom's old room. She does it in secret, although I have no idea who she's trying to be stealthy from. Maybe Grandpa Roger? I dunno. The room is kept as a shrine, something I remember from the last time I visited. Kurt Cobain rules the walls with Courtney Love in tow. I sit on the bed and can smell my mom, even though it's been years since she's likely been there. Childhood bedrooms have a way of trapping scents.

"I'm worried," she says, bringing a shaking tissue up to her nose and giving a light blow.

My heart stills. "Yeah, me too."

"She hasn't checked with Grandpa Peter at all," she continues, eyeing Cobain and Love on the walls, as if they're to blame for Mom's disobedience. "He's all right, but it's cruel of her not to check-in, just cruel that one."

I take a gulp. "Do you have any idea where she could be?"

Her eyes cut over. She shakes her head. "It's no secret that your mother and I have not been close in some time, ever, really. She…we see life so differently." She nods, agreeing with her diagnosis.

"I'm reading her journal, her diary, whatever it is," I say, but Grandma Luanne isn't paying attention.

"I'm not sure what more I could've done. She ran away after her sister died—you know that. And then she found music, so we supported that." She blows into the tissue again, but nothing comes out. "We let her join the band, live with her boyfriend, your father." She throws up her hands. "She was barely older than you. But her father and I decided that she was happy and hadn't been in some time, so who were we to tell her no?"

"I think it was really cool that you let her live her dream."

Grandma Luanne takes my hand, squeezes. "Thank you, Love. And of course, that led her to having you, but I'm sure you know, we didn't believe she was ready to be a mother. And that's...that's..."

"When she started to spiral?" I ask, my mouth so dry. "Dad said she was very depressed. Did she have postpartum?"

Grandma Luanne shoos that thought. "Oh, well, she went to plenty of doctors. And we paid for rehab."

"Rehab?"

Grandma Luanne squeezes my hand harder. "Yes, Love, she had addictions. Alcohol. I went to Al-Anon. They tell you it's a disease and not to be angry, but I have anger, I really do."

"Did rehab help?"

"Rehab...well, it was a bandage for a time. And the therapy too. Problem was we had already lost her by then. She was gallivanting around—you know she made a lot of money off of that first Evanico record. Used it to travel. She was always somewhere in Europe, and she was a full adult by then, so God-forbid she'd listen to any advice from us. The years just went by. Occasionally there would be a call, but nothing more.

She's a stranger, Love. That's what she is."

I'm staring into Cobain's soulful eyes. "So, what's different now?"

She gulps a breath. "What's different now is that there'd been a reconciliation between us over these last months with her father ill. She was doting, concerned, I mean, in her own way. We were working toward something. And then, nothing. Just cruel that one."

Grandma Luanne picks at her short gray hair. I wonder why most old women cut their hair so short, except for Carly who lets it roam. I already miss staying with her.

"So…" I begin, unsure how much I want to say, but the train's already left the station. "Part of why I came to L.A. was to see you of course." Grandma Luanne gives another thin smile. "But I also want to talk with people from Mom's life to see if she was in touch with anyone before she…vanished."

Grandma cocks her head to the left in confusion.

"Like, like her friend Winter…"

Grandma Luanne makes a sour face.

"Or Jeremy, ya-know her close friends from high school? I was gonna reach out to them."

Grandma Luanne flicks her hand. "I don't know how much that'll do, but knock yourself out."

"Jeremy owns a hair salon, right? I think my mom has said it's in Malibu?"

"You can use the computer if you want to search."

"And Winter? Do you know anything about her?"

"Divorced," Grandma Luanne spits. "Has a child about your age. Husband's name was Fang or something horrible like that."

"What's her last name?"

"Her mother still lives not too far away. Occasionally I've seen her in Gelson's. Edina, that's the woman's name."

"Do you remember where she lives?"

"Not far from the dog park. Amor Road. Just knock on the door of the house that smells like marijuana."

"Luanne!" I hear from downstairs.

Grandma Luanne pinches her sweater closed and goes to the door. "What?"

"The kids want more cucumber slices," Grandpa Roger bellows.

"Don't you know how to use a knife?" she calls back. No response. She throws up her hands.

"Useless, just useless," she mutters, and heads downstairs.

I'm left alone in Mom's room. I go over to her CD, press play and "Shine" by Collective Soul comes on. The last song she played here. I see a collage of pictures up on the wall of Mom with Dad when they were young, Mom with Winter looking stoned, and Mom with a blonde girl when they were super young, probably Kristen. There's one solo pic of Mom dead center. She's on a stage with red lines outlining her body, her hair a shimmering blue. She's scowling into the mic, sweat pouring from her face. Her eyes filled with pure delight.

I pluck that picture off the wall and keep it as a memento.

She was happy once.

She could be happy again.

14

• • • • •

SOMEBODY'S WATCHING ME – ROCKWELL

January 16ᵗʰ, 1998

It's been over a week since I've left Evan and Love. I'm in a cabin surrounded by land and not much else. There's a fireplace to keep me warm and a little restaurant down the road that serves English style food, bangers and mash, beans on toast, blood sausages. The owner is an old English woman who reminds me of Winter's mom, and I'm glad for it since she's kept my belly full. I sit in the cabin and have taken up knitting. All day at the window I work on a sweater that's slowly forming. The sleeves are off, but it will suffice.

I have guilt for leaving them both but knew that I wasn't doing them any good sticking around. I left a note, which told them not to worry. I said I would be back because I do want to be back with them. I just need to get myself right before I do. Leave this funk that I've carried along for so long.

I'm surrounded by mixtapes, songs I've loved over years that will bring me solace. I have Grenade Bouquets' album and Evanico's too. Listening to them, it's hard to believe that it's my voice. That right now all over the world people are hearing me too. That I could be helping them through tough times. I bet they would never think that I needed help too.

The goal is to reach a place where I can record again. I miss putting pen to paper, but ever since Love was born, my quill is dry. I should be inspired by her, by my newfound role. I hold onto the theory that distance makes the heart grow fonder and that my heart will come around. This was a speed bump and nothing more.

I know Evan hates me right now. Probably wonders how his life took this turn. I picture him fleeing back to Idaho so his parents could give him a hand with Love. Cursing them, cursing me. But something is not right inside of me. My brain isn't working like it used to. And I'm trying, I'm really trying. I'm not a monster. I could be loving, mothering. A hiccup's preventing me from getting there, and I just need to figure out what that hiccup could be. Then I will be fine. Nico again.

So, I sit by the window listening to old grunge music from years past and knitting this sweater. Surrounding me is the woods. Dark trees that take on forms when the sun sets. It's nighttime when I feel most alone and usually make my way down to the restaurant for my meal of the day. It's the walk back that I fear the most. In the country, every sound amplifies. Animals abound. But people barely exist. There's a tiny town on the other side of the restaurant, farther from my cabin. A post office. A bank. A grocer. A few small homes, trailers. But no one would need to keep walking past the restaurant toward my cabin. That's the appeal.

But yet. I've been seeing someone. First, I noticed them late, late at night when my eyes were so sleepy, I could've been dreaming. Flitting between the shadows stood another shadow. It moved every-so-slightly so I knew it wasn't a tree. Trees tend to sway in the distance, but not move. This moved. The shadow then darted across the field. I could hear its feet pounding against the grass before it disappeared into the night. I looked at the joint I was finishing and figured that must be the culprit for my vision. But then it happened again.

This time I was walking back from the restaurant, Addie giving me a to-go bag with a ham and butter sandwich for the next day. There was the shadow, silent but tangible. It stood between two tall trees, its arms moving as if it was waving at me but not in the way like it was saying hi—it was beckoning me. So, I ran. Dropped the to-go bag with my sandwich and booked it back toward the cabin. Got under the covers in bed and shivered until I managed to fall asleep.

The next day, I searched for the sandwich I'd left behind. It was bitter cold but hadn't snowed, so I figured it would be easy to find. The to-go bag was there, but the sandwich had been eaten, the wrapping left over. Sure, an animal could have done it, however an animal wouldn't have unwrapped the sandwich so carefully. It likely would've eaten the wrapping too. I was convinced someone was watching me.

It happened again a day later. This time, I made sure to forgo any joints so I could stay sober. And then, at night I heard a rustling sound as if someone was scraping their nails against the cabin's walls. I grabbed a flashlight and went out to check. That night it was snowing. Tiny flakes causing a ruckus. I could barely see. Chilled to the bone, I investigated. I'd see a shadow disappearing around a corner of the cabin, but when I'd get there, it was gone like a puff of smoke. I went back inside and sure enough the scraping sound started again. Louder this time, nails on a chalkboard. I grabbed the flashlight and jumped outside, screaming this time, challenging this shadow. But nothing, only the moon watching, a sliver, until it vanished behind a thicket of clouds.

Now I was even more frightened because I rationalized that I was losing my mind before I got here, but *for real* losing my mind now. I had to get out of here. If someone was after me, I was a sitting duck in this cabin. Although, they hadn't attacked yet. They enjoyed watching me, and maybe, that's all they wanted to do. Watch. Observe. Be close to me.

I couldn't call Evan, and I hadn't spoken to my parents in too long, so that would've been awkward. Carly would listen, but I needed someone who could come up with a plan. I dialed Winter, the connection spotty. She was getting serious with this guy Fang, but when she heard the fear in my voice, she listened. She told me to get the F outta Dodge. What was I doing in the middle of nowhere? I should drive down to L.A. and we could head somewhere, anywhere I wanted to go. Fang would give her the days off, no problem. I asked her if she thought I was being watched and she hesitated. I know she thought I was crazy and didn't want to say it, so she just repeated to get to L.A. If I drove all night, I could be there by morning.

So, I hung up the phone, threw all my stuff in a suitcase, journal and half-knit sweater included, and slammed on the gas. Flying out, something, a presence, banged on the trunk of my car as I left. Through a quick glance in the rearview, I could see the shadow, but it wasn't a shadow anymore. It was a man. Tall. Thick. His face masked by the night, but he was yelling at me. Waving his arms and picking up his pace as he ran after me. I floored it, weaving down the small, dark road, past the restaurant and the nothing town until I could see him no more. I kept driving until I reached Winter in L.A., not even stopping to pee and wetting my pants twice.

When I arrived soaked, she let me cry on her shoulder, put me in the bath, and then we were back on the road before the sun rose.

She played Rockwell's "Somebody Watching Me", maybe as a joke, and I told her "too soon, too soon".

15

• • • • •

BLOWIN' IN THE WIND – JOAN BAEZ

On our way to Grandpa Peter's and Annette in Los Feliz, we take a detour to stop by Winter's mom Edina. Driving down Amor Road, I think of Grandma Luanne saying to just go up to the house that smells like marijuana. Frankie and Caden are exhausted from Grandma Luanne—and let's be honest—I am too, so they want to nap in the car while I investigate the block. There's only about a dozen houses, so potentially I could ring each doorbell, but one house in particular looks different, an odd pink amongst the rest. Going up to the door, I hear Joan Baez's version of "Blowin' in the Wind" and take a chance that it must be Edina.

I ring a doorbell and a woman with a sea of frizzy orange hair the color of Sunkist opens the door with a funky-looking cigarette stamped between her lips and a floating caftan hanging off her thin body. She has tiny eyes that blink in awe.

"Nico?" she says, and then shakes her head. "No, it can't be."

"Hi," I say, weirded out by the way she seems to absorb me with her gaze. "Are you Edina, Winter's mom?"

"Yes, of course, child." She sucks the funky-looking cig. "Of course, of course, you're Love, right? But why…?" She angles her head out of the door and spies Frankie and Caden snoring in the car, frowns. She must've thought I was with my mom. "Oh."

"Yes, it's me," I say, sounding stupid. "Love."

She puts her hand on her hip. "Well, Love, you come in why don't you?"

Her home smells of patchouli and Grandma Luanne was right—marijuana too. She goes over to a record player and lowers Joan Baez. I think of how similar she and Great Aunt Carly are—how they'd likely be friends. That even though Mom's mom was so different than her, she found these alike souls in other women.

"Well, let me look at you," Edina says, squinting her eyes. "A beauty. Just like your mom. How is she?"

I sit on her couch, fold my hands in my lap. "That's why I'm here."

And my eyes start swimming with tears. I need to stop, but I can't. Edina sits next to me, hugs my shoulder.

"Oh, child, don't cry. What's bloody wrong?"

"She's missing," I say, grabbing a tissue and blowing. "My mom, she vanished."

"Hmmm."

She puts out her funky-looking cigarette and puts on a serious face.

"I was going around to people she knew, seeing if anyone heard anything."

"Well, no. I haven't seen your mother, it's been some years. Such a lovely voice though. I have all her music."

Edina gets up and brings over the Grenade Bouquets and Evanico CD.

She points at the Grenade Bouquets CD. The cover a literal bouquet of grenades about to explode. "This one was a little too loud for me, but Evanico was my jam."

I manage to laugh at her calling it her "jam".

"Has she been in touch with Winter, your daughter?" I add, as if she doesn't know that Winter is her daughter.

"Don't know. She might've. Winter lives Downtown where she has a store too." And then under her breath, she whispers: "Skid Row."

"Oh."

"Oh, it's not like that. Very up-and-coming area if you like that thing. She has a daughter your age, you know?"

"Yeah, I think I heard that."

Edina rolls her eyes. "We're having a row now. I always seem to get on her wrong side. So, I couldn't tell you exactly when she last talked to your mother. Missing you say?"

"We don't know. She was in Europe, but no one's heard from her in about two months."

Edina rubs her arms as if she's gotten a chill. Then her face changes from concerned, to perky. "Oh, she'll turn up. I'm sure. Don't you worry. Don't you cry, Love. You really look so much like her."

"I know, everyone tells me that."

Edina grabs a Post-it, a pen, and scribbles. "This is the address for her store, best place to find her. Her number is always out of service, so I wouldn't bother with that."

I take the Post-it. "Thank you. Are you two gonna be okay?"

Edina takes a deep breath. "I gave her too wide a berth," she says. "Same thing happened with Nico. We let them roam, fall into their own mistakes. I was raised differently so I swore I would be looser but look what that did. Both she and your mom with a child as a teenager. Can you imagine?"

I cover my stomach in fright. "No, definitely, not. No thanks."

Edina's lip twist into a smile. "Good girl. So, both of them grew up too fast. And for that, I'm regretful. They were wild girls, but we should've had a tighter leash. You know, I've seen your grandmother in Gelson's and neither of us has anything to say. It's been fifteen years since the girls were teens, but it's like she's embarrassed. We know our shortcomings better than anyone. Although, I'd die for my grandbaby and I'm sure your mother would die for you. Winter too. She's a wonderful mom. Not the easiest person, but has that maternal instinct, even though Delilah's a handful herself. I guess we all are in our own ways."

I clutch the Post-it. "I'm gonna see her after I visit my grandpa. Thanks again."

"You think nothing of it, darling."

I head to the door. Her eyes creamy and sad.

"Edina, have you ever told Winter what you just told me?"

"Well, no, I...not in those words."

"Maybe it could help? For her to hear it. Like, to

be acknowledged in that way."

It takes her a second, but eventually she nods. "That's a good point. A good point, Love. You're a good girl." She comes closer and gives me a hug.

"And she'll turn up," she says. "Your mom. She's a good girl too."

16

• • • • •

TORN – NATALIE IMBRUGLIA

Driving to Grandpa Peter's, things are a bit awkward with Frankie and Caden. We haven't really spoken much, since Great Aunt Carly dropped her bombs. That in our trio, Frankie ruled the roost and Caden and I are basically in love with her. So, we listen to the rest of the Jeff Buckley album and then switch to a mix CD with jokey songs like "Torn" by Natalie Imbruglia. This had always been me and Frankie's favorite to make fun of, lip syncing at each other from across the room, and then pretending like some terrible thing tore us both apart. Now it feels all too real.

"Okay, I'm just gonna talk because I can't take the silence anymore," Frankie says. She's sitting shotgun while I drive, making her hand into an airplane out of the window. I see Caden look up the rearview, his forehead full of worry lines. "Do either of you feel like 9021-*Hole* is not an equal friendship between all of us? Because I really think it is. Yeah, I might talk the most of the three of us, but that's doesn't mean I'm the leader or anything."

"I don't think that," I say, and Caden nods.

"Maybe I can be more aware," she continues. "I dunno." A car passing by honks at her, and she gives them the finger. "God, I hate L.A. traffic."

We all agree on that.

"Let's just have fun," I say, lowering the music. "I mean this is our summer break, and I've dragged you both out here while I play detective. Despite all that, we can still have a good time."

Maybe I'm feeling a little more energized after I talked to Edina. We still had Winter and Jeremy to potentially give an insight to my mom's whereabouts. Hope isn't all lost.

Frankie gives a sly smile. She cranks up the music and starts singing "Torn" at the top of her lungs. I croon along and we mime Natalie Imbruglia's most desperate feelings. Even Caden drums against the back of the seat. When the song ends, it seems like we might be back to normal.

"Seriously," Frankie says, "if I'm ever monopolizing the convo too much, let me know."

"And," I add, "if this trip ever becomes too much about my mom, let me know too. I want it to be great experience for all of us."

"Deal," Frankie says, and we do our special hand-shake where we punch fists and blow on our thumbs.

"Turn right for your destination," the GPS says, and I pull up in front of Grandpa Peter's ridiculous mansion that seems plucked out of a silent film. We get out and drag our suitcases up, ring a doorbell that plays "Fur Elise". We're met with Annette who greets us in a short bob like Betty Boop, wearing fire-red lipstick, a hefty dose of rouge, and a turtleneck that's probably way too warm for June in L.A.

"Ah, come in, your grandfather's napping," she says, sweeping her arm and beckoning us into a grand foyer with a staircase that twists up into the clouds. Paintings that could be in museums hang on the walls and the floors are made of marble and have an echo. Annette has a successful restaurant that's been in the neighborhood for over twenty years, but the real money came from Grandpa Peter, who used to work in finance before he retired.

"Whoa," Caden says, and then clamps his hand over his mouth.

Annette winks like she knows her house is rad.

"Love, you were just a child the last time you were here," she says. "I remember you trying to slide down the banister."

A phantom pain in my crotch surfaces from remembering that attempt.

She plants three kisses on my cheeks like we're in Europe. "It's so good to see you."

"You too, Annette. And these are my friends Frankie and Caden."

Annette waves. "You'll each have a bedroom upstairs. Let's get you settled and then I'll wake your grandfather."

"How's he's doing?" I ask, hesitant.

Annette steels herself. I imagine she's perfected being strong during his illness. "He has his bad days and good ones. But the good ones are starting to outnumber the bad, so there's that."

She swivels and ascends the staircase, prompting us to follow.

Later, after we're *settled*, we hang out in a room she calls the parlor room while she fetches Grandpa Peter. It takes a long time, and we occupy ourselves with the little trinkets and do-dads that probably cost as much as it does to put me through college.

Grandpa Peter rolls in in a motorized wheelchair. He's far from the grandpa I remember, his hair entirely white, with wrinkles deep enough to wedge a finger, and skin that seems to hang off his bones. He wears slippers and his feet are so white, I can't look at them, but then I have to look at them.

"Love," he says, his mouth twisting to the side. Annette stands close by, her hand on his shoulder as if she's feeding him her energy.

I introduce Frankie and Caden, who are polite and shake his hand. A butler, or whatever he could be called, looks as old as time, marches in with tea sandwiches. I grab a few with smoked salmon and capers and get to munching.

"So, your mother," he says, his mouth sagging into a frown. Then he shakes his head in disgust.

"Peter…" Annette coos.

"No, Annette, she has *no* regard for the people who love her. Never has. Spent her life gallivanting off. A shame."

He whisks a tea sandwich from off the butler's silver plate and starts gumming it.

"You look so much like her," he says.

"Yeah, I know," I say, getting tired of hearing that.

He points at Frankie and Caden. "And the same

friend circle. Boy and a girl, no other friends."

We look at each other, and I can't deny that he's right.

"Lemme ask you," he shouts at them. "You give your parents hell?"

"Peter," Annette coos again. "They're good kids."

"Drinking and drugs, that was how your mother spent her time."

Annette slaps his arm, but playfully.

"We don't do that," Frankie says, with half a tea sandwich in her mouth. "We're straight-edge. I mean, we don't exactly say we're straight-edge because, like, we don't need to identify with a group, but we're about a natural high."

Grandpa Peter stares back at her like she's just spoken an alien language.

Speaking of aliens, I use this as an opportunity to probe.

"Grandma Luanne was talking about rehab and therapy," I say, and watch as Frankie and Caden recede into the wallpaper. They know to take a backseat when I'm playing detective.

Grandpa Peter flaps his hand. "Yeah, yeah, nothing ever stuck. You know, she had pain, your mom. We all did. When Kristen died…"

He looks out the window like he's trying to see her in a cloud passing by.

"It changes you, no matter what. And she was so young. And I was always gone, working."

He throws up his hands, showing what his work has paid for. A lifetime chained to a desk for a palace in Los Feliz.

"You can't blame yourself," I say, because it's what you have to say.

"Oh well."

I get up from a *frou frou* couch and take Grandpa Peter's hand. He's stunned.

"I'm gonna talk to her old friend Winter. And Jeremy, do you remember them?"

Grandpa Peter gives a tired shrug.

"I'll see what they might know. That's why I'm here, a window into her past that could give us a clue. We'll find her, we will."

I'm smiling so wide that he has to do the same. He manages a half-hearted grin followed by a coughing attack into a monogrammed handkerchief.

"It's the paranoia," he says, after he gets it under control.

"What?"

"The paranoia, that's the worst of your mother's troubles. Used to think she was being watched."

I'd read the diary entry where she had mentioned the same thing. Alone in a cabin, a shadow stalking. I'm guessing it wasn't only that time.

"A shadow," I say, and his eyes go big and bloodshot.

"Yes, yes, a shadow. She would always complain about a shadow."

"Did she say anything more specific—"

But then Grandpa Peter's coughing attack gets worse, bringing up major mucus from the depths of his soul.

"All right, all right, Peter," Annette says, in her sing-song way.

I'm torn, dying to ask him more, but I don't want

to kill the man.

"Let's get you in the steam room," she says, as if having a steam room in your house is the most normal thing. He nods at that.

"Why don't you all use the pool out back?" she says, and then turns around wheeling Grandpa Peter out before we can respond.

"My mom wrote an entry in her diary about a shadow following her," I say, to Frankie and Caden once Grandpa was gone.

"I think it's time to see her friend Winter," Frankie says, tossing a do-hickey in the air. "You talked about making sure we have fun this trip. To me playing detective is much more fun than a dip in their boring pool."

"I agree," Caden says.

I shove a final tea sandwich down my gullet. "All right, let's track down this Winter."

17

• • • • •

WHAT'S UP? – 4 NON BLONDES

January 17ᵗʰ, 1998

Wiiiiinnnttterrrrr! I can't tell you what it means to see my eternal Ride or Die. After the nightmare in the cabin either chased by a shadow or my diseased mind, she's exactly what I need at this moment. She's living with this dude Fang in a wreck in DTLA that looks out over a woman screaming into a garbage can, but I love it. We sit on her stained couch while Fang cleans up empties around the dark apartment. He's a big dude full of tattoos and I don't think I saw him smile once, but Winter seems gaga for him, so who am I to get in their way? They make out as they say goodbye, swapping way too much spit but it's kind of sweet. I don't remember the last time Evan and I kissed like that. We morphed into an old married couple thanks to Love, and I miss our innocence.

When we leave, it's nighttime, no destination in mind. I came from up north, so we head south, maybe San Diego across the border into Mexico. We're armed with a mixtape that blasts the 4 Non Blonde's "What's up?" and we shout it out of the windows at all the passerby. I don't want to think about Evan, or Love, or my next album that's due. I want to be a teenager again, since I'm about to turn twenty and then I'll be dried up.

It's been about a year since I've seen Winter and so much has changed. She's a chiller version of herself. The dreads are gone, her bone-white hair cut short and dangling on her shoulders. She has a sippy cup full of alcohol and we pass it back and forth. It tastes of Kool-Aid and grain punch. I'm driving and I know I shouldn't be doing this—I'm a mom now and it's irresponsible to potentially crash into a tree, but I don't care. I say hey, hey, hey, hey what's going on? What's going *on* is that I'm losing myself and need Winter to help me get back to the Nico I used to be—free.

In San Diego we stop at a bar close to midnight and whip out our fake IDs—Sasha Lioni my alias still brings me all the luck. I'm worried I'll be noticed, but I put my hair up in a bun, which should fool any clinging fans. There's a dance floor by the bar and 4 Non Blondes comes on, and we're screaming. I know the song is everywhere, but we *just* heard it. I've never been more in the present moment than dancing with Winter as if no one is watching.

"I love you, Wint," I tell her, and seal it with a friendly kiss. She tucks my hair behind my ear and wipes away my tears.

"Oh, Nico Nicotine," she says, with a pout. "I love you always. Remember how we've talked about doing wheelchair races in the retirement home? That's us!"

"Vroom, vroom."

I'm crying even more and shaking in her arms.

"But why cry, sunshine?" she asks.

"I feel like I'm not in control."

We reconvene at the bar, and she gets us beers because she says that beers help settle your emotions. I sip the foam and am surprised that she's kind of right.

She wipes away a beer mustache. "I know what you mean, girl. I've lost control again and again. Remember the Zedd AIDS debacle?"

Do I ever. Canceling tour spots and rushing to be with Winter when she thought she contracted HIV from her on-and-off boytoy Zedd. Zedd and Fang, where does she come up with these dudes?

I shrug. "But I'm a mom now."

"Yes, and Love's being looked after by Evan right now. She's safe."

"Evan never would've done what I've done. Just take off."

"Evan's not a star like you." She bats her eyes. "Burning so bright, too bright sometimes."

"I'm trapped in Eugene. The walls. His breath. Love's cries. I can't think."

"Just because you had a baby with him doesn't mean you have to be together."

"True. But it's not just him. It's her. She's so needy."

"Duh, she's a baby."

"I never thought a baby required so much sacrifice. I sometimes wish..." I lower my voice. "I don't even want to say it."

"You regret having her?"

"I wish I thought about the consequences more. Because—this—what I'm doing now. *This* is my runaway, my one runaway. I can't keep doing it again and again."

"Why not? Maybe that's you, the runaway girl? Not the first time you've done it, ya-know? You're a nomad, Nico. A wanderer."

I stretch out my mouth as I say, "Wanderer."

"You can't be contained. I can't either. Some have tried. Your parents, Evan, now Love, now Fang for me."

"Are things getting serious with Fang?"

"He makes my knees quiver."

I picture Fang's linebacker body on top of me. I try not to wince so she doesn't take offense.

"I'm happy for you."

"And you," she squeals. "You're a Rockstar. You've shared a dressing room with Jewel. You don't have to color in the lines. It's in your DNA not to."

"Yeah?"

"Yeah, Nico, don't feel bad for anything you do. Would it better for Love if you stayed at home miserable with her?"

"No."

"Then there's your answer. Fly bird, fly, flap your wings."

She spreads her arms and knocks this guy in the head. The guy's drink goes flying all over her and they start cursing. The guy pushes her, and Winter pushes back. Then I get involved and clock the asshole across the face, taking out all my aggression. I'm pummeling him enough until people are pulling me off of him and the bouncer gets involved and we're held until the police arrive. We're tossed in the backseat of a patrol car and brought to the local drunk tank where we're placed in separate cells across from one another, singing "What's Up?" through the bars because we're too afraid to go to sleep on the shitty mattress and get bed bugs.

When we're let out in the morning, the sun is a bruise and I'm hungover and the smart side of me would take this as a sign to go home, but the idiot that has a hold over my decisions floors it south still, picking up greasy Jack in the Box to-go, and crossing the Mexican border in San Ysidro.

It's in Mexico when things go hazy. I know it involves Tequila and a nasty worm and we drink too much and I'm tasting the floor. Feet dance around me, but I don't care. I puke and it's different than I've ever puked before, this burns with the intensity of a thousand fiery suns. Then I'm in a hospital and the lights are so bright and it smells horrible, and my stomach is killing me. I'm yelling for Winter, but she's not there, probably yelling for me herself wherever she wound up. Everyone is speaking in a different language and I can't understand them and I'm scared and I want to be back at home with Evan and Love more than anything. I want to feel safe. But I know that I'm no good for them in this way.

So eventually when Winter and I find each other, shivering and in old clothes from the night before covered with hardened puke, we drive back in silence. No tunes playing either. I let her off in L.A. and we give each other a weak hug, saying it was good to see her but knowing that we're honestly bad for one another. I can see it in her eyes, the exhaustion. We could've wound up dead. Maybe that's what we wanted.

I know I won't see her again for a long, long time.

When I get back to Eugene, I drive right up to a rehab clinic and check myself in.

18

• • • • •

HAZY SHADE OF WINTER – THE BANGLES

Winter's store in Downtown L.A. is called Vs., a nod, I assume, to Pearl Jam's second album with an angora goat on the cover. Sure enough, when we enter, a blown-up poster of the album greets us along with fashionable clothes from the 1990s. I see a slip dress with plaid on the bottom and a leopard print on the top that I take off the rack. Frankie gives a thumbs up and I do the same for a sweatshirt dress she spies. Caden's got a vintage T that says *Hi, how are you The Unfinished Album, Daniel Johnston 1983* with an alien print made famous by Cobain. We planned on each buying an item and approaching Winter that way, rather than bombard her with questions about my mom.

A girl that looks college-aged mans the floor, no way that can be Winter. I took the picture of my mom and Winter from her bedroom before I left Grandma Luanne's house, and not only does this girl not have white hair, but she's also about fifteen years too young to be Winter.

"I can ring you up," she says, as if she could care less.

I hand her the slip dress. "Uh, ok."

She slouches to the register, scans the dress. One hundred and fifty dollars! I hadn't even looked at the price.

"Uh, I didn't realize it was so expensive," I say.

She sighs with daggers from her eyes. "You don't want it?"

"Well..."

Frankie and Caden join me by the register. They don't have the clothes in their hands anymore, smart enough to have looked at the price tags.

"Is the owner of the store here?" Frankie asks.

The girl turns her daggers toward her. "Why?"

Frankie gives this sweet smile she does when she really means murderous rage. "Old friends."

The girl picks up the phone and presses a button. "Winter, someone's here to see you. I dunno. Friends? Like children? Okay."

She hangs up the phone. "So do you, like, still want the dress?"

"Who is it?" I hear from behind me and swivel around to Winter. She's wearing a tank top with a badass black leather jacket, Doc Martins with the laces tied around the top of the boots, and aqua blue eye shadow. Her hair is still bone-white like in the picture, snapping gum, her lips maraschino cherry red.

She stops in front of me, a laugh at the back of her throat. She knows. The resemblance obvious like everyone says.

"Well, I'll be," she says, her hand on her hip. "You're Love, right?"

I'm suddenly super shy, can barely stutter. "Yeah."

She dances over, flips my hair, takes in my duds. "Spitting image of your mom. Like, so cool. Delilah looks nothing like me. I wonder sometimes if they switched babies in the hospital. C'mere."

She pulls me into a hug, smelling of cool perfume.

She's looking around. "Is your mom here too?"

"Uh, no, that's why we came. These are my friends Frankie and Caden."

Winter gives a jazz hand wave. "I like the posse."

I take a deep breath. "My mom is missing."

• • •

Winter takes us out for iced coffees down the block at a cool café that kinda reminds me of Café Hey. There's a stage set up for Open Mics and good desserts like Marjorie makes. I realize I need to give my dad another call soon and shoot a quick text that we've made it to Grandpa Peter's now and are having a really good time.

"Hazy Shade of Winter" by the Bangles starts to play, and Winter laughs. She has this machine gun type of laugh that goes on and on but it's really endearing. She's singing under her breath.

Our coffees are served, Winter drinking hers black while we get ours loaded with the works.

"When was the last time you saw her?" I asked, taking a huge sip. The sugar firing right into my brain.

Winter chews her lip. "A while. We've been bad about keeping in touch. I mean, it happens. You guys in high school, like your friendships are *so* important at the time and then life takes over."

I look over at Frankie and Caden and my heart drops. We hadn't spoken about where we'd go to college, but the odds were against us all going to the same place. Senior year would be the last chance we'd really spend together.

"So maybe about a year ago. She was down in L.A. It was super brief." Winter takes a sip of her coffee. "She was seeing a show, I think, but then left before."

I lean closer, as if she just gave a clue. "Why did she leave before?"

"How much about your mom do you know?"

I whip out the journal and show Winter. "I'm getting to know her a lot more."

Winter fingers the pages. "Holy shit. Her journal, man. I mean, I haven't seen this in forever. Have you read the whole thing?"

"I'm up to the part where you both went to Mexico and she came back to go to rehab."

I see Frankie tap Caden on the shoulder and nod for him to get up. They both rise.

"Let's leave you two alone," Frankie says.

"You don't have to," I say, really wanting her there.

"We'll take a walk. C'mon, Caden."

When they leave, I feel less centered, like I'm made of air and could just float away.

"Mexico," Winter says, with a frown. She takes a long sip of coffee like she needs it. "What a disaster."

"Yeah, mom wrote about going to jail and then the hospital."

"Jail wasn't bad. We sang 4 Non Blondes all night

there, kept each other sane. The hospital on the other hand… Both of us had our stomach pumped. It was a wake-up call for me."

"Really?"

Winter picks at the end of her hair. "Oh yeah. And when I came home, I was still feeling weird, so I took a pregnancy test. Boom."

"Oh, your daughter?"

"A blessing in disguise. At first, I was like, fuck no. I mean, I had plans, ya-know. But I was with Delilah's father at the time, and he was all into it. We were gonna buy an RV and live on the road." She looks to the right, likely imaging that different path her life could've taken. "He cheated on me, typical. And then he felt… constrained, that was the word he used. So, he left."

"I'm sorry."

"I'm not. My fault for choosing a man named Fang to be my baby daddy. He's actually not too bad. He calls Delilah from time to time. They have this like buddy-buddy relationship. Takes her to Lakers games when he's in town. So, it could be worse."

"What do you know about when my mom went into rehab?"

Winter sucks on her teeth. "You seem like a sweet kid. Really. Head on your shoulders and all. Your mom would be proud."

"You don't have to sugarcoat anything."

"Yeah, I know. I hear ya, girl. I was the same. Like *hated* when adults treated me as clueless, but I'm not sure you need to know everything about your mom from those days. Wasn't pretty times."

I pat the journal. "It's all here. I already know. I

just want to hear a different perspective."

She taps on the table. "Okay, and just so you understand, I don't know everything. That's when she and I started to go our separate ways. We... I think we saw the danger in our friendship, how we could push each other to the edge. So, we cooled down. Yeah. But she was in rehab for a long time. Like, almost a year, I think. I visited once."

"What was she like?"

"She was different. I mean, she'd been sober so that was good. She didn't tell your father where she was, even though it was right in town; her parents either. I like, got a call one day, and then I was in my car driving up to Eugene."

I stir my straw to give my hands something to do. "So, how was she different?"

"Besides being uber guilty about leaving you? She really was. I'm not making that up. It like, gutted her. But she was afraid to leave the facility."

"Because she'd start drinking again?"

"No. Well, I'm sure that was in the back of her mind. But she was convinced someone was following her."

My heart stops. I have to actually feel my chest to make sure it's still there.

"Wait, she wrote about this in her journal."

"Yeah, I'm not surprised. It messed with her. I don't know if she thought it was a crazy fan..."

"She was the in the woods," I say, raising my voice and then calming myself down. "And there was this shadow..."

"Yeah, yeah, a shadow. She always talked about

this shadow. So, the facility didn't wanna release her. Until she stopped thinking she was seeing things. And I do believe she felt safer there."

"Do you think she was telling the truth?"

I'm nervous to hear her answer to this question.

Winter strokes her chin. "I believe she really believed what she saw. And maybe she did have a run-in with someone who freaked her the fuck out and just couldn't let it go. She wasn't ready for the kind of quick fame they had. Grenade Bouquets got a little famous, but not like Evanico. That was a year of being everywhere. You couldn't get away from seeing her face. I was jealous, I admit. I was."

I swallow hard, taking in this information.

"Maybe she saw this shadow again and that's why she took off?" I suggest.

Winter gasps, shows me her arm. She has a tattoo of a dove.

"Goosebumps, Love, look. You gave me goosebumps."

I rub my hands over my own arms, feel goosebumps too.

She grabs my hand, probably realizes I look scared.

"Hey, I'm closing up shop soon anyway for the day. Come back to my place, you can meet Delilah. Let me think about places she might have gone."

"Okay." I sniffle, a tear trickling down. I wipe it away.

"It was a hazy time back then," Winter says. "But if I shake up my mind enough, maybe something'll fall out."

19

• • • • •

DIRT – ALICE IN CHAINS

January 20ᵗʰ, 1998 – till whenever

So, rehab. I could've gone back to Evan and Love, sweated it out at one of my parents' abodes, but I wanted anonymity. In a clinic, on an off street in Eugene, I'm no one. Nobody cares I had an album in *Billboard's* Top Ten, or did a duet with Jewel, or shared a cigarette with Courtney Love, or am a daughter, a girlfriend, a mother. The days flip by, indistinguishable. I don't have the need for alcohol, or weed, or my new friend over the last year, E. I was never addicted. Only addicted to leaving my body, this Nico Sullivan who everyone requires something from. My entire goal to escape her.

Here at Tomorrow's Another Day, I achieve that. I go to the group meetings, the one-on-ones with a counselor, the therapy that digs into my issues. Did those issues start with the death of my sister Kristen? No, I was fucked up long before then. They put me on meds, change the dosages, fiddle around to attain the right equilibrium. Moving from one kind of drug to another, but these okayed by Big Pharma, so it's justified. Do I feel better? I'm not sure. I feel less. Less angry, less sad, less needy. More like I just seem to drift. From room to room, meal to meal. I socialize but everyone's dealing with their own shit and we all bathe in that attention. Jockeying to see whose problems outweigh each other. Death, destruction, adultery, prison, a flatline, kids taken away, a shoot-out. Some of the patients are younger than me but have lived full terrible lives. Abandoned as children, living on the streets, sex for food, a dog as their only friend. My heart breaks because they make me feel like an imposter.

The center is run by a woman named Lucille, who is literally brought down to Earth by angels. Lucille gives every inch of her to us. She is our tough mother, our warm embrace, the only being in this world who seems to understand. Nothing is our faults. We each had a disease. We each need support to be stronger.

Lucille keeps a cigarette pack in her sleeve like a 50's greaser out of a James Dean movie. Life has ridden her hard, her face telling that story. Wrinkles like troughs. Cigarettes her only vice. "At least they'll kill me slowly," she coughs. I catch her outside in the backyard, ripping at a cigarette so hard she finishes it in two sucks. That's talent. She calls me the voice. She encourages me to sing. "But for yourself," she says. "At least for now. Sing for your heart."

Every morning I'm encouraged to wake up with a song. She told me to go down the list of my favorites. I pick the grunge songs of my youth. I love how I can speak of "my youth" like I'm old and bedridden, when I'm really about to turn twenty. I sing Nirvana, I sing Pearl Jam, I sing Soundgarden and STP, Soul Asylum and Garbage. I sing Alice in Chains "Dirt" so often I dream the chorus. My suitemate Molly likes it. She's pretty much mute. Something wrong with her tongue. Part of it is missing, I don't know. She's never fully smiled. But she receives my voice, gets out from under the covers at least.

I leave a message on both my parents' answering machines. I'm not sure if they're home and don't want to pick up—their lives easier without me mucking it up. I've given them the freedom they've always desired. Or maybe they are really out. I tell the machines that I'm all right, not to worry, that I'm taking some time for *me.* With Evan, I don't have the nerve to call because he'll pick up. So I write a letter. The early version is thirteen pages of me cracking open my cranium. The version I send is one sentence, broken up. *I am okay, please don't worry, I'm taking some time to get healthy, I'm sorry.* Mailing it makes me throw up that entire day.

I'm not writing songs because they trigger my downfall, but I am reading a lot of poetry. Classics I never paid attention to in high school from the clinic's library. Dylan Thomas and Emily Dickinson. Wallace Stevens and e.e. cummings. I try my hand at it as well. I'm terrible.

But. I am getting better. Digging through the mud to return to a Nico I like. She's there, hidden by brick that can be chipped away. I'm chipping. And then.

A setback. Lucille warns us all the time. Recovery is not a straight line. "It's like the stock market, up and down, up and down. But you never sell. You ride it out." Easy to say but difficult in practice when you're in freefall territory.

I see my shadow again.

I'm in my room, it's late at night, and a shadow creeps up the wall. Normal, right? Shadows are everywhere. But when I go to investigate, someone, or some*thing* is stalking from across the street. Watching. Hidden enough from the moonlight so I can't make out a face. Is it a man or a woman? A being from another universe? We're not allowed outside after dark, so I'll never know. Like clockwork, it appears right before I go to bed. I tell Molly but she's too afraid to look, she's frightened of everything. I mention it to Lucille but by the time she arrives in my room, her sigh tells me everything I need to know. The shadow is gone. She points at the empty street as evidence. "They're hiding!" I shout. "It's all in your mind," she responds. "Let's change your meds." We alter said meds, but the shadow always returns, crafty son-of-a-b. I come to accept its presence. We are bound now. But at least in these walls I am safe. It's when I'll leave that I'll be in danger.

Lucille recommends that it's time for me to be discharged. At some point, I need to see if I can make it in the outside world because I can't live here forever. I can always come back, though. I beg her to let me stay longer. I bring up the shadow again. If I'm imagining it that can't be good, right? She says the shadow has become my crutch, my Linus blanket. I don't know what the hell that means.

Still. It buys me some time while they adjust my meds a smidge more. I'm dying to see someone other than the same patients over and over, so I call Winter. We haven't spoken since our stint in Mexico. I'm worried she no longer wants to be my friend. That we've realized we're each other's bad influence. But she drives up all the way from L.A.—that's love. She's a few months' pregnant but barely shows with her rocking body. She seems more centered, a dulled version of the Winter I knew, but a more rounded one at the same time. She's glowing. She's beautiful. She's exactly what I need.

However, when I tell her of my shadow, she recedes. She doesn't believe me, I can tell, and I know that scares her. She repeats that there is no shadow, and I get upset because the shadow is a reality to *me.* Whether or not it's real, it doesn't matter. Winter pats my hand. She sees how upset I am. She wants to be there, but we're still fucking teenagers and don't know how to deal with these major kind of problems. We've had to grow up so fast.

"Don't you want to get back to Love?" she asks, and I break down in tears. My obsession with my watcher has taken away from my focus on Love. I've put her aside. I'm a terrible mom.

Winter calms me down. She tells jokes. She plays the jester. I manage to laugh, mostly to make her feel better. Before she leaves, we hug for a time, like she knows she's my lifeline. She makes me promise to call her any time I'm feeling "screwy".

I pinky promise. But don't talk to her for a while

because something happens.

I'm throwing out the trash just before dusk because it's one of my chores and I'm attacked. It happens so fast I don't even realize that someone has their hands on me before I'm thrown onto the ground. I become the Tasmanian Devil, whirling around and striking my pursuer, running away back into the clinic with proof of a gash on my wrist. They believe I cut myself. My medications get super changed and I become a zombie. I exist only to do basic human functions, and I have no idea how long this lasts. But I don't see my shadow anymore. It seems to have disappeared.

Slowly, I become engaged again, friendly, sweet, even sarcastic—my go-to. My meds are reduced. I leave my zombie state. It's winter again and there's snow outside. I wake up one morning singing Alice in Chains "Dirt", but I no longer want to melt into a mushy puddle. I want to attack the day. Really sing again. Create songs. Be alive. And more importantly, I feel a fierce desire to see Love, and hold her, and whisper how sorry I am, to Evan too. I want to tell them I'll never leave again.

Lucille says I'm ready. It'll be a trial. I'll take a few months away from the clinic. She encourages to reach out to some of the people in my life again. Test the waters. Be kind to myself.

I leave with a Jansport knapsack and hail a yellow cab. When the driver asks me for my address, I tell him "my family's home", Evan and Love—that is if they'll have me.

We'll just have to wait and see.

20

· · · · ·

HEY THERE, DELILAH – PLAIN WHITE T'S

My mom's friend Winter lives in a grungy apartment in Downtown L.A. by her store. She says she can't beat the commute, which is her way of surviving in a city where most people spend over two hours a day sitting in traffic. We climb a stairwell to her place on the top floor that has a long hallway separating her and Delilah's room. I can hear rock music coming from her daughter Delilah's wing and I like her already.

"Let me go wake the beast," Winter says, rolling her eyes and disappearing down the hall.

Frankie, Caden, and I sit at a counter in the kitchenette where a sink overflows with dishes. Candles are scattered throughout the apartment, lit to the nub. A huge on-brand (for Winter, from what I've gleaned) poster of a Pearl Jam show is framed above the mantel, clearly the star of her abode. Curtains drown out the incessant sun that I'm already starting to lose patience with since we arrived in California. I miss Eugene's weather where it could rain at any second.

Winter comes out from down the hall with Delilah in tow. Delilah's our age but tall as a supermodel. Her hair is black and shorn one end and blonde and spiked on the other. She wears raccoon eye shadow, and her clothes all have rips in them. But in a super fashionable way. She has headphones around her ears like she can't part with music for a second and seems less than thrilled to have to make small talk with us.

"Delilah," Winter says, pushing her toward us. "This is Nico's daughter, Love, and her friends Frankie and Caden. You remember me telling you about my old friend Nico, the one in a rock ba—"

"*Mom*," Delilah says, dragging out the word in a whine. "Yes, you've told me about her a billion times."

Winter waves her off. "Anyway, I'm gonna go change. Delilah, raid the fridge with them."

"Great," Delilah says. "We can all split that one orange you keep."

"There's Pizza Rolls."

Winter leaves down the hallway before Delilah can say no, singing "Hey There Delilah" by the Plain White Ts, surely to get under Delilah's skin. We enter into a staring contest of who's gonna give in first. Finally, Delilah opens the fridge and gets out the Pizza Rolls.

"Gross," she says. "It's pepperoni. Like could my mom be any unhealthier?"

"I'm not hungry," I say, because I will not put processed garbage like that or meat in my body.

"She's so lame," Delilah says.

"She actually seems kind of cool," Frankie says, Winter's new defense attorney.

"She likes to *act* cooler than she is," Delilah says.

"She does that with everyone who comes over. The chill laid back mom. It's fake."

"Yeah, my dad does that too," I say. "Like he's one of the gang."

"Is that what you are?" Delilah asks, with a smirk. "A gang?"

"We're 9021-*Hole*," Caden says.

Delilah's face gets screwy. "What the fuck does that mean?"

Frankie butts in. "It's a mixture of our two favorite retro things—*90210* and Hole. Love is named after Courtney Love."

Delilah flips the hair on the blonde side of her head. "That's actually rad."

I grin like a fool, enjoying the compliment. I'm surprised that I want her to like me so bad, that I even care about what a girl other than Frankie thinks.

Delilah chucks the Pizza Rolls in the trash. "So, what are you all, like, doing here?"

I clear my throat. "My mom went missing and we're visiting people in her life to see if they have any clue where she went."

Now Delilah perks up. "That's awesome."

"Really?"

"I mean, not that your mom is missing, but that you're playing detective." She flops on a leather couch. "I am super bored. I'd totally help."

"Really?" I say again, sounding too eager. Frankie gives a look like *calm the hell down.*

"Sure, who were you seeing next?"

"Do you know Jeremy? I don't know his last name."

"Uh yeah, Uncle Jeremy, like of course I know him."

"He's your uncle?"

"He and my mom are still way close. I see him all the time. He has a hair salon out in Malibu."

"Yeah, that was gonna be our next destination."

Delilah gets closer to me, whispers. "You know, he's closer to your mom than with mine. They've really kept in touch. With her and my mom it's just once in a while. I think it makes her jealous."

Winter emerges from the hallway. She's wearing tight jeans with high heels and a cool tee with graffiti-style writing. She's moussed her hair, slicking it back.

"Stop talking about me," she says, with a wink and bumps Frankie on the hip.

"You look great, Winter," Frankie says.

Winter gives a twirl. "This old thing. I have a happy hour date."

Delilah's eyes go to the ceiling. "Mom, no one wants to hear about your sex life."

"Oh, Delilah, what do you want me to do, dry up and die? I'm in the prime of my life."

"Who's the date?" I ask.

"Thank you for asking, Love. It's a third date. His name is Ray. He's an entertainment lawyer."

"Mom, no one cares!"

"Love and her friends do. Anyway, you think this is okay? We're going to this after work drinks spot."

"Spot on," Frankie says. "He's a lucky guy."

"You all are too sweet." She sticks her tongue out at Delilah, who sticks out her tongue back. Then she comes over and rubs my arm. "So, I was racking my brain if there's anything else I could think of about your mom's whereabouts. Her friend Jeremy..."

Delilah pops up. "Mom, you are twelve steps behind. We've already discussed Uncle Jeremy and I'm gonna take them to Malibu."

"Oh. Well, I'd go with you if it wasn't for my date."

"Go on your date," Delilah says, grabbing a purse off the coffee table. "This conversation is already boring."

"Jeremy and your mom kept in better touch then she and I did," Winter says, sadly. "Your mom and I...there was always a competition in our friendship, trying to outdo each other. With Jeremy it's just easy. If Nico told anyone about where she went, it'd be Jeremy."

"Good to know," I say.

She dwarfs me with a hug. "Oh, Love, it was so good to see you."

"Mom, stop being weird!"

Winter is still hugging me. "Nico created such a perfect daughter with you. I know she's so proud."

I'm trying not to well up. "You think?"

"I *know*. Even if she doesn't show it, she's in awe of you."

"Mom, enough—"

"Unlike the spawn of the devil I birthed from my loins."

"Mom! Ugh, we're going."

Delilah grabs my arm, leading me out the door, Frankie and Caden following close by.

"Good luck," Winter yells. "And keep in touch, Love. It was great meeting you."

Over my shoulder, I can see Winter waving as the door slams closed.

21

• • • • •

FAR BEHIND – CANDLEBOX

December 28, 1998

I tried to make it work, I really did. First with Evan and Love, then with my folks. I admit showing up at Evan's after all this time without an explanation may not have been the smartest idea. He was pissed, to put it mildly. Screamed his head off at me while Love cried in the other room. He wouldn't even let me see her. Said he moved in with his family for a while until that was too much of a disaster. Assumed he'd be a single dad for the rest of his life. No one knew where I was. Astral Records wouldn't leave him alone and eventually severed the contract. After almost a year away, I'd been presumed dead.

After he calmed down somewhat, he let me explain. It was hard, believe me, because I couldn't really put into words why I left.

"I just felt like I'd tear out my hair if I didn't go," I said.

"Was it me?"

"No! I mean, yes. But not you personally. It could've been anyone making me feel this way."

He gave a laugh. "Glad I mean so much to you."

"Can I see her?"

He hesitated, then beckoned me into her room. She was sleeping in a crib, but so big. A tiny nugget when I left and now a girl with short hair and footy pajamas. She was perfect. I longed to hold her, but knew I wasn't strong enough yet.

We sat on the couch in the living room and I attempted to explain what happened. How I wasn't able to control my sadness. How fame and the responsibilities of being a new mom were too much to handle. He listened but I wasn't sure he believed. He still thought I was being selfish.

He let me sleep in the spare bedroom. The next day I woke while he was giving Love breakfast and she was smiley and happy with baby food all over her face. I watched from afar, not ready to join. He was kind and patient with her. He was who I wished I could be.

Each day was a slow reemerging into this old life. I'd sleep a lot, which Lucille said was normal. I'd repeat mantras into the night to boost my confidence. I'd inch toward Love again. Maybe feed her the first time, change her diaper, take her for a walk in her carriage in the blustery weather. Evan and I didn't speak much. We weren't ready to work on our relationship yet. It was all about Love.

But I wasn't Mama yet. I was an entity that existed in the house to her, but there was no certainty I'd stay. So it was hard to give her love. I wasn't sure if I had love in me. A few weeks in, I spent an hour staring at her, begging myself to feel it, the powerful, crushing swelling of doing anything for your child. But I was still numb.

"It's too fast," I told him one rare snowy day when we were stuck inside. "It's like I'm forcing a feeling."

"God forbid I force you to love us," he said, throwing up his hands.

"That's not fair," I said. "I'm doing my best."

"Your best isn't good enough. And it's not *fair* to Love."

I left that night when he was asleep. This time was even harder than the first because I figured it was for good. I didn't need to go back to the clinic. I hadn't had cravings for alcohol or drugs. I needed my parents, more than I ever needed them before.

This was an even bigger mistake.

My mom welcomed me, but it was hard to fit in with her new life and Roger: the two of them newlyweds and me this sour grape. I could see she was getting fed up, avoiding me at all costs. I'd be turning twenty-one soon—a full, full adult. She wasn't required to mother me anymore. She'd lost whatever maternal trait she once had—and I couldn't blame her because I was the same.

Dad and Annette were better at first, since we found it easier to leave one another alone. Both of them so busy with work, I'd rattle around the big house alone most days.

But that was when my shadow returned.

I'd been doing well, at least in regards to the shadow, but then one day I'm staring out of my bedroom window at the back lawn—which had become a favorite pastime of mine—and stalking between the trees my shadow emerged. This time it wore a hat tilted down over their face, non-descript clothes all in black. Menacing eyes tilted up toward my window, and I ran into the closet.

Dad and Annette found me hours later, my pants wet with urine. I was a crazed beast, yelling about my shadow—I even described the eyes this time—but was met with shakes of their heads.

It was all in my mind. There is no shadow. Blah, blah, blah.

I heard them discussing me that night. The house so big it echoed. I watched them from the top of the grand staircase as they threw out words like "bi-polar". They questioned the clinic I was at. They wondered about others. Dad would make some calls in the morning. I feared the type of place I'd be shuttled off to with a lunatic label taped to my back. Even though I was frightened of the shadow in the night, I fled their house in my nightgown, getting in my car and driving... where to...?

I couldn't think of anyone who'd want to see me, not Winter, only...Jeremy, who lived on the west side of L.A. with a boyfriend now. We'd lost touch but he'd never turn me away. I was sure of it.

So, I floored it down to the beach blasting Candlebox's "Far Behind" and singing along. I hadn't sung since the clinic, and I missed using those muscles.

I rang his doorbell sometime around dawn, nervous that if he'd didn't accept me, I'd have nowhere else to go but to fling myself at the ocean and let it carry me far into the blue chopping waves until I'd vanish and become nothing more than a story once told.

22

• • • • •

MALIBU – HOLE

Jeremy's place in Malibu, *Hair*! near Zuma Beach, is packed when we arrive. Rock music pumps from speakers and hairdressers whirl around in an all-glass space that overlooks the ocean. The girl at the desk, Purple, has (surprise) purple hair and immediately recognizes Delilah when we all walk inside.

"Delilah," Purple gushes. She reaches across the counter to finger Delilah's sculptured hair. "Love what Jeremy did the last time. Looking for a change?"

"Thanks," Delilah says, friendlier than I've seen her act thus far. "Actually, just stopped in to see Jeremy and introduce him to some family friends."

Purple eyes us up and down. "You all looking for a cut? He's a little busy, but I can squeeze you in with Blue and Magenta while you wait."

"Yes," Frankie says. "Please fix these split ends!"

Frankie and I get our 'do's done side by side while Caden and Delilah go for shampoos.

"Delilah seems cool," I say, as Magenta snips at

my bangs.

Blue measures how much of Frankie's hair to chop off.

"I guess it's nice of her to bring us here."

"I've been reading more of my mom's journal too. Gnarly stuff."

"Like what?"

"Rehab, a clinic, her parents saying she was bi-polar. She really had it rough when she had me."

"Voila!" Magenta says, giving one last snip. It's shorter than before, curled at my shoulders, a little shaved on one side like I asked, since I thought Delilah's looked good.

"Perfect," I say, eyeing myself in the mirror. I'd certainly date me.

Purple comes over. "Looks like Jeremy is done with his V.I.P. He's in the break room."

Frankie and I nod. Her hair looks great too, actually clean since she rarely gave it a good wash. It's feathered and poufy and brings out her blue eyes.

I gulp. "You look amazing."

Frankie gives the bottom of her hair a bounce with her palm. "This ol' thang."

Caden and Delilah come over with wetted towels around their shoulders.

"Hey, Frankie," Caden says, twisting his toe into the floor.

"Uh...hey, Caden."

She gives me a look like he's crazy.

"I really like your hair," he murmurs.

"Okay, thanks, buddy," Frankie says, leaping out of the chair.

Delilah puts her hands on my shoulders. "Yours looks bitchin' too. Like the close shave."

I'm smiling big. "Really?"

She runs her fingers through the side of her head shaved close too. "You know it. C'mon, let's go see Jer."

In the breakroom, we hear Hole's "Malibu" coming from under the doorjamb. A definite favorite of mine.

"Uncle Jeremy," Delilah says, knocking as she opens the door. I'd seen one picture of Jeremy before, a skinny kid with baggy jeans and frosted blond tips. In person, he has long fire-red hair, coiffed to perfection. He's wearing an oversized chunky cable knit sweater and jeans that look painted on with loops and tassels hanging from the sides, high-tops on his feet, diamond studs in his ears.

"Deee-Lite," he screams, jumping up and giving Delilah a hug and then air kissing. "What brings you to Malibu? Touch up?"

"Actually..." Delilah says, and gestures to me to step into the light. When I do, it's Jeremy's eyes that light up.

"Stop," he says, hand on hip. "I know exactly who you are. A baby Nico. Oh, it's like looking into a way back machine."

"Hi," I shyly wave. He air kisses me on the cheeks as well.

"And your mom?" he asks, glancing around the room like everyone's done after seeing me. My stomach drops. He has no clue she's missing either, meaning she has no idea where she went.

I go through the whole spiel, leave no stone unturned. He responds by walking over to a mirror with a brush and applying some blush.

"I've found that there's no situation that blush doesn't make a little better," he says. "You know," he continues, pointing at me with the brush. "Your mom has wanderlust. She can't help it."

"When was the last time you spoke to her?"

"A month." He taps the blush on his chin. "Maybe two? Hard to tell. We get so busy at *Hair*!"

"How did she sound?"

"Normal. I mean, normal for Nico."

"What did you talk about?"

"I'm afraid it was mostly about me. I was going through a horrible break-up with my on-again-off-again. We've been together in some form since I was at Vidal Sassoon back in the nineties. He's an addiction, the worst kind. But I love him!"

I feel like we've come all the way for nothing. "So, she didn't talk about herself at all?"

"She was in France. Nice I believe. That girl loves Europe. She thinks Americans aren't free enough. Ironic because we're the *land of the free*. But she means free in a take-off-your-top-and-run-along-the-beach way. *Verboten* to Americas. This place stifles her."

"You think she's still in Europe?"

"Not likely, I remember her passport or Visa was expiring. Something along those lines. She mentioned coming back to the states because we were gonna try to get together. It had been—well, let me see now—three years since I'd seen her last. Too long."

"But she didn't say where in the States?"

"'Fraid not, chickabee. You know your mother ran

away from home when she was your age? Not that I'm advocating for you to do the same. Maybe she's doing that again?"

I haven't thought of that. Of mom returning to her youth by duplicating the journey she took after her sister died.

I'm getting excited again that she might not be missing after all, just on an extended road trip. "Where did she go then?"

The CD starts skipping, so Jeremy walks over and bangs the player on its side. Hole continues with "Celebrity Skin".

"God help me, CDs are the worst, but I just can't make the switch over to iPods. I'm a full album kind of girl, ya-know?"

"Totally," Frankie says. "I'm a CD 'ho too."

"I like this one," Jeremy says. He closes his eyes and rubs his temples. "Lemme think. Okay, she started in San Luis Obispo. She always wanted to climb a mountain and faced her fear there."

"San Luis Obispo," I say, sounding out the words.

"Then she went to Muir Woods," Jeremy says. "Where she got arrested." He lowers his voice. "You didn't hear that from me."

I hold up the journal. "I think I've read worse about her."

"Ooooh, her old diary. If these pages could talk. Anyway, she was arrested for protesting deforestation, nothing too scandalous."

"These are really good leads," Frankie says.

"Yeah, thank you so much," I say. "Maybe she is recreating her runaway. Running back to the past when it was a simpler time for her?"

Jeremy shakes her head. "It was never simple for that girl. Especially when Kristen died. Maybe going back to all those old haunts helps remind her of Kristen? Might be worth a shot?"

"It's all on our way home anyway," I say. "We just have to convince my dad."

"Oh, how is Evan?" Jeremy asks batting his eyes. "How she let a good man like that go to waste is beyond me."

"He's good. I mean, he's worried about her too."

Jeremy puts his hands on my cheeks. "Sweetheart, you don't worry. That cat has nine lives and more. She's gonna land on her feet. Just you watch."

"Okay," I say, trying not to cry for the billionth time.

He kisses my forehead. "Okay. And you all be sure not to pay for your cuts today. On the house. It was lovely to finally meet you, Love."

"Ditto," I say.

He claps his hands. "All right, break time is over. My VIP is waiting for her dye to set. I'll give you a hint, it's Cher—"

"Holy shit. Cher!" Frankie gasps.

"Cher's number one drag queen impersonator, Turna Backtime."

He starts cackling.

"Oh dears, you thought I meant Cher. I'd never put her on blast that she dyes her hair. Doctor-patient privilege. I'd take that to my grave, sweetiekins."

23

. . . . .

AS LONG AS YOU LOVE ME – BACKSTREET
BOYS

December 29th, 1998

"Nico Nicotine!" Jeremy yells, before tackling me with
a hug at his door. I'm flummoxed, not knowing what
to expect. It's hella late in the night, and I haven't
talked to him in forever. I always think that someone
might not care about me anymore if too much time
has passed. And so much time has gone by with old
people from my life that I worry they've forgotten and
moved on.

"Jer Jer," I say, my smile forced, because I'm still
losing my mind from the shadow stalking me and
feeling adrift.

We do this little dance we used to do that mimics
Kid N' Play where we touch our feet together, grab
other by the arms, and spin around. I can't tell you
how much I needed it at that moment.

"Well, you look..." he begins, then stops. I look a

mess and there's no way of sugarcoating it.

"Like a werebeast," I say, pointing to my cuckoo crazy hair as evidence. The last time I ran a comb through it, God only knows.

He waves. "Come, come in."

Jeremy's got a cool bungalow by the beach in Venice with a window overlooking the boulevard and drum circles. I've missed the L.A. air, a whiff of beach with a hint of smog and rot. It smells too clean in Oregon. Too many trees to eat up the fumes.

"Lo is sleeping," he says, with a finger to his lips. Lo being his boyfriend with the clothing store JAZZ. Lo who pays for the rent. Lo who's about a decade and a half older. "He's a sound sleeper though. Let's go to the den. Yes, bitch, I have a den!"

His "den" is tight. A huge TV with a PlayStation hooked up and a giant poster of that guy in the Pepsi commercials with Cindy Crawford, sans shirt, abs on full display. There's a tiny bar and he goes to make a drink.

"I'm good," I say, shaking my head.

"Right." He chomps his teeth. "Rehab. So, like, it worked?"

I tear up, emotions too tough to bottle up with Jeremy. His sweet face with cropped ultra-blond hair, roots beginning to show, and a Backstreet Boys tee.

"No more Chris Cornell?" I say, wiping those tears away.

"I mean, I'm always a Cornell girl at heart," he says, tapping his heart. "But I wouldn't kick any of the Backstreet Boys outta bed, especially A.J."

I hadn't been listening to this new boyband craze,

too busy losing my existence. Besides, I don't think it would be for me anyway.

He turns on Backstreet Boys and starts lip syncing the words to something called "As Long as You Love Me". Retch.

"I suppose you wanna know why I'm here?" I ask, so he'll turn down the music.

"We can talk about whatever you want." He's petting my hair. "You know that."

I go into the whole spiel. Evan, Love, rehab, the shadow, my meds. I jingle some around in my pocket as proof.

"That's heavy," he says, mixing Crystal Pepsi into his cocktail and then kissing his fingers. "Divine."

I throw up my hands. "I don't know what to do. I don't know where to go. I don't know who I am."

"Girl, you can reinvent yourself at any moment. All of us can. Look at me... No one spoke to me in high school, except you and Winter. Now I'm at Vidal Sassoon, living on the beach with my dream guy."

"You love him?"

"We fight like hell, but that keeps it spicy. He's a Scorpio, need I say more? But when it's good, it's so good. You and Evan never felt that way?"

"Yeah, I mean when it was good it was really good too. But not for a while, not since Love." I hide my face in my hands. "I'm a terrible mother."

"Who says?"

"The world says. I've seen the magazines."

I have not, in fact, seen the magazines but could only imagine they were crucifying me.

"Those people mean nothing. You're a star, they

always go to cap your knees."

"Nice Tonya Harding reference."

He holds his palm up like he's praising Jesus. "You know I pray at her altar. Stupid Nancy Kerrigan."

We both agree on that.

"I just don't think I'll ever have my shit together," I say. "If the shadow is real, then there's a crazy person who wants to harm me. If not, it means I'm the crazy one. I don't know what's worse."

"Girl, of course you're crazy! Anyone who touches greatness is. Being boring is the worser tragedy."

We both agree on that too.

"Like what did your rehab place say about this... *person* following you?"

"That it was in my mind. All the pressure built up. The drugs, alcohol, stardom, Kristen dying, my parents divorcing. We went through *every*thing in my life till I was nauseous."

I hear a knock on the door as it swings open. Jeremy's boyfriend is there: rumpled, greying at his temples. He looks like an absent-minded professor rather than the owner of a hot boutique. Blessfully, he turns down the Backstreet Boys.

"Baby, it's late," he says, purposefully glancing at his wrist as if a watch was present.

Jeremy jumps up and does a tap-dance. "Baby, this is Nico! Lo, I told you about her a bazillion times."

Lo squints. "Right, right."

"I'm so sorry we woke you," I say, starting to get up. I'm embarrassed, and I want to leave. "I was in a crisis."

Jeremy slaps his thigh. "Nico is in a crisis. Lo is

the best for crises. Nico, tell him what you told me."

So, I go through the whole spiel again, and Lo's eyes light up when I tell him about my stardom.

"Oh, right, the friend who's the singer," Lo says, frowning at Jeremy. "Jer, you should have led with that."

"I'm sorry, Lo, this is my very, *very*, extraordinary famous friend Nico Sullivan of Evanico."

I shake my head. "Evanico is no more."

"Oh, shame," Lo says.

"It's my ex," I say. "My baby daddy. We're not really speaking."

"Hence the crisis."

"If that were my only crisis."

"Right," Lo says. "Well, what's the most pressing one right now?"

I look around. I feel safe in their den. That the shadow isn't watching. But outside? By the beach amidst in the drum circle? Stalking, waiting. I'm sure of it.

I slump my shoulders, defeated. "I feel like someone is after me."

"I might know someone—"

Jeremy claps his hands. "Davina!"

"Yes, Davina," Lo says. "She's a witch. But a good witch. Promise."

"O...kay."

"Davina has ways of casting off evil spirits."

"Do you think that's what it is?" I ask, sounding so small.

"You think of spirits as something tangible," Lo says. "But they're not always. It could be a ghost, but it might be a trauma you've had and the hurt of reliving it again and again."

Lo stands, satisfied with his answer.

"The root of all your problems is this. It's inhibiting you from a relationship with your ex, your daughter, your fans even."

"But I felt this way even before the shadow," I say, scrunching up my face.

Lo wags his finger. "No, this shadow of yours was always there. It was just waiting for the right time to strike. And it has, honey. Let me tell you it has!"

"Where's this Davina?" I ask.

"She's in Venice too," Lo says. "She'll be awake now. A witch like her lives by the moon." He winks at me. "Come, come, girl. You came all the way here, let her read your leaves."

"Let's do it!" I say, standing up with him, confident. This gives me a hope, even if it's a small one. I'm willing to try anything to be normal again.

Jeremy squeals. "The gang is back together." He gives me another strangling hung, the alcohol on his breath poignant. "I mean, not Winter. But we swapped her out for Lo. It's just as good!"

24

• • • • •

WALK ON THE OCEAN – TOAD THE WET
SPROCKET

Traveling back through all my mother's old haunts
was a brilliant idea of Jeremy's to try and locate her.
We decide on San Luis Obispo as the first spot, since
that was where she initially went when she ran away.
From there we would go up the coast to Muir Woods,
and then Portland and Seattle before ultimately heading
home. Only problem is—my dad. He thinks we'll be
staying the entire time at my grandparents' houses and
I really don't want to lie to him. He doesn't deserve
that. So, I call, no idea what I'm about to say.

"Hey, Love, it's good to hear from you. I try to be
cool and not bother you, but ya-know, I want to call
every five minutes."

"I texted."

"I know, and you've been good at that. I really
appreciate it."

"How's Eugene?" I ask.

We're outside of Jeremy's hair salon—Frankie, Caden, and Delilah waiting in the car. I have my toes in the sand by the beach while I make my flip-phone call.

"Oh, Eugene is the same. Nothing changes much here."

"And Marjorie?"

A few seconds of silence. "She's…she's actually over right now. She's been spending a lot of time here."

Again, I'm torn between sharing my dad with another woman and also being glad he's found someone. I repeat to myself not to be a dick about it.

"Good, that's awesome you both are getting along so well."

"Really?" He sounds surprised.

"Yeah, really. Definitely, Dad. She's nice and cool."

"That means a lot, Love. And you, how's the trip going? You behaving?"

"Totally. And yeah, it's been a…trip certainly. Good to see Grandma and Grandpa, but I need to be honest with you."

"Uh-oh, what's this about?"

I stare at the ocean, its vastness. How the sky seems to vanish into its waves.

"I came to L.A. to search for Mom."

Dad doesn't respond right away, only clicks his tongue. He sometimes does it when he's stalling.

"In L.A.? Honey, I don't think she's in L.A."

"No, I wanted to talk to people from her past who maybe had a clue where she went. And so, I saw her friends Winter and Jeremy. Jeremy had an idea…"

I could tell he's not pleased. "Okay…"

"So, she ran away one time, right? That was when you both met. It was right before she became famous and maybe she wants to relive that time? Jeremy told me about all the places she went to, and honestly, it's on the way back home. So, I thought—"

His sigh burns my heart. "Love, I don't want you to get your hopes up."

"I'm not! I mean, I wanna try at least. What's the harm? It's making me feel closer to her. The first stop is in San Luis Obispo—"

"I'm not a fan of you driving around the country—"

"Dad, it's on the way home. It'll just take us a little longer to get there. Winter's daughter wants to come along. We can do it all over two to three days."

"Wait, you're friends now with Winter's daughter?"

"Yeah, Delilah, she's awesome. Like really awesome. And she really wants to help."

"Okay... I mean, but where are you gonna stay?" Now he's put on his Stern Dad Voice.

"A hotel?"

"No, no, this is too much—"

"Listen, I didn't have to tell you. I could have just—"

"Just what, lied to me? I would've found out that you weren't staying with either grandparent, and you would've been in a fuck lot of trouble."

"Right, but I respect you, so I told you."

"That doesn't mean I'll let you get away with whatever you want."

"Dad!" I'm seething now, regretting my choice to keep him in the loop. "This means a lot to me. I've gotten to know her—Mom—throughout this trip. I know I was a burden to her."

"You were not a burden..."

"Don't try to deny it. She wishes she didn't have

me. I was the start of everything going wrong in her life. You two breaking up, the band as well. None of that would've ever happened if not for me."

Surprisingly, I'm not crying. I've accepted who I am and what I've done.

"Love, you're not responsible for anything that happened to your mother. She does this all the time, at least she did. She allows others to take the blame for her mistakes. She is the parent, remember that. And she gave me you. I can't imagine my life without you. You are by far that best thing that has ever happened to me. Her not wanting to be a part of it is *on her*, no one else."

"She thought she was being followed, Dad. She had issues, mental ones, but I don't think she ever got the right kind of help. Let me do this. Please. We'll be safe. We'll be home in a few days. I can charge a motel room with your card and the four of us will look out for each other."

"What if I say no?"

I swallow hard. "Then I'll go anyway."

• • •

There was a lot more back and forth before I was able to convince him, but finally I wore him down. I said I needed to do this not only for Mom, but for my own sanity, so I could feel like I did everything possible to find her. He couldn't argue with that. He wanted the number of each hotel we'd stay at and to text when we'd arrive and when we'd leave. He made sure that everyone else would get permission too. I agreed to everything.

Taking off from L.A. after the rest of our gang called home and got the okay for this detour (Caden's took the most convincing, both Frankie and I speaking to each of his moms and assuring them that we'd be safe and check in every hour), we're finally driving with the windows down, Frankie in shotgun, and Delilah and Caden in the backseat, super free in a way I've never experienced before. We have three days straight of no adults physically watching over us, but more than that, I sense I'm closer to my mom than ever before. At one of the points along our upcoming journey, she waits. I just know it.

We arrive in San Luis Obispo and park by Pismo Beach to scour the area. I picture her trying to learn surfing, crushed by a wave but finally landing one and gliding.

"What does your mom like to do?" Delilah asks, and I shrug.

"Seriously, I have no idea. Jeremy said she came here to learn how to surf."

Caden starts pacing around. "Those waves look really big."

We watch a surfer flip upside-down from an in-coming wave.

"I'm *not* doing that," Caden says.

"We don't have to surf, but maybe someone saw her?"

With her picture in hand, I ask around the beach but no dice. We decide to get veggie burgers and fries and milkshakes instead."

"So, let's say you find her," Delilah asks. "Then

what?"

I choke on a gulp of strawberry milkshake. I hadn't thought about that. Maybe deep down I really believed I might never find her.

I'm chewing on my lip. "I guess find out why she left."

Delilah's eyebrows turn down. "You think she'll tell you?"

I shrug again. This is making me feel like we really don't have a plan at all.

Delilah takes the last bite of her burger. "What do you want from her?"

This I know the answer to. "An explanation." I'm frustrated and I push away the rest of my food. "Something, anything."

Delilah puts on her sunglasses, and I stare at myself in the aqua mirrored frames.

"If you ask me—" Delilah begins, but Frankie butts in.

"No one did."

Coolly, Delilah keeps going, unfazed. "You're searching for her because something is missing from your own life." She gazes around. "Each of you."

Frankie slams her fries. "You seem to have a *lot* of opinions. Don't you have anything better to do than tag along?"

Delilah crosses her arms. "Not really. I was bored. I'll admit that. I wanted a break from my mom for a minute. What are your excuses?" She points at Caden. "You do whatever they tell you."

Caden looks away, embarrassed. Delilah turns her attention to Frankie.

"And, you—"

"I'm her best friend," Frankie chirps. "We'd do anything for each other. Maybe you don't have that and that's why—"

Delilah throws her hands up. "You don't have to get defensive. I'm just asking questions. Okay, you all find her mom, then what?"

We look around the table at one another, no answer to give.

"Maybe I could write songs, like her?" I mumble, surprised at myself for even saying this. "Like, learn how she does it."

Frankie glares at me across the table. "You've never told me this."

"I've tried it sometimes," I say. "Just scribbles. I don't tell you everything."

Now her glare becomes like ice. I have to admit that I like pissing her off. I've been thinking about our dynamic and the hold she has over me. Who makes those rules? She enjoys her superiority because of how I feel about her and that I know she might never reciprocate.

"I'd love to read one of your scribbles," Delilah says.

Now Frankie really gets her knickers bunched up.

"C'mon, Caden," she says. "Let's take a walk."

When they leave, Delilah inches closer. "Your friend likes to make a big deal about things."

I watch Frankie and Caden become dots against the shore.

"She likes being possessive," I say, and then immediately want to take it back. I've never spoken bad about Frankie like this before, but to be truthful, there's been no one else to be honest with. It's been the three of us in 9021-*Hole* for so long.

Delilah rubs the shaved side of her head. "You like her." She says this like a statement.

"Well, of course. I mean, she is my best friend."

She smirks. "Like her, *like* her."

"No, I mean. I dunno."

"It's cool. I mean, I'm fluid. I don't really think about gender. Or gender constructs. Even labels."

"I've only kissed a boy...once," I tell her, almost hiding in my hands.

"Did you dig it?"

"No... He was a bad kisser too."

"First kisses always suck. Mine was terrible. He slobbered all over me like a puppy."

"What about girls?"

I can't believe I'm asking this. She's looking at me funny too. Like something could happen. I'm aware I'm sweating like hell, my pits a downpour.

"Girls are more tender," she says, looking to the left and probably remembering all the experiences she's had. "But they could be bad kissers too. The trick is a little tongue but not too much. Let the tongue be a good surprise."

I go to sip my milkshake to give me something to do, but it's empty.

"Wanna try?" she asks, and before I can answer she's kissing me. Her lips plump and soft and tasting of strawberries. I let her open my mouth slightly with her tongue and get this funny feeling in my stomach. She begins to pull away, but I'm still reaching out like I want more.

"Did you like that?" Delilah asks, giggling.

All I can do is nod. I liked the way it felt, sure, but still don't know if I like *liked* it. Maybe I don't need to make it so complicated. Maybe I can just enjoy the moment.

"Let's play some tunes," she says, and angles her phone as "Walk on the Ocean" by Toad the Wet Sprocket fills the air.

I can still taste her on my lips.

Frankie and Caden return. Caden with a huge shell he's proud of and Frankie with a sour face. She's upset, I can tell. She's threatened by Delilah.

Maybe I'll tell her about our kiss, just to see her reaction. Just to see if she wishes she'd been the one to have kissed me first.

All I know is I want to put all of it down in song lyrics: this moment, this rush—and I've never had that desire before. Maybe I do like girls, or maybe I'm born to be a songwriter and today's my birth.

I came to San Luis Obispo with the intent of finding my mom, never expecting I might find what's been even more lost—myself.

25

· · · · ·

SOUL TO SQUEEZE – RED HOT CHILI
PEPPERS

December 29th, 1998

Davina the good witch lived in Venice Beach as well,
closer to the drum circles. Even in the middle of the
night, the drummers beat wildly, playing for the almost
full moon. Her house is full of crystals, (Aunt Carly
would've approved), along with enough plants to turn
it into an arboretum, the earthy scent like we stepped
into a bog. She has chanting with music playing, the
same dirge over and over, like a blessing. The door is
wide open as if she knew we were arriving.

And then, on the stairs, she emerges, her frizzy
hair in a headwrap, her body a mix of old and young,
hard to tell. She has a presence as she glides down
the stairs, as if light beams from behind her. I know
it's the reflection of the moon, but it seems like more.

"Davina," Lo says, with a wave. He stands straight
and rigid like she'll correct his posture. "We brought

a friend."

She tilts her head back like she's balancing an imaginary object on her chin, very Daisy Buchanan—the last book I read in school being *The Great Gatsby*.

"Yes," she says, making it clear she knew we were arriving. "This one," she continues, her cool hands on my cheeks—I'm blushing. "You came because you needed my help."

I gulp. She can see right through me. I've never felt more naked.

She leads us into a grand room with ivy crawling up the walls. Her face lit more now, no makeup but a goddess, like each feature was exquisitely crafted. Her long nose, pouty lips, skin like alabaster. If you told me she was from another planet, I would've agreed.

"How is the relationship?" she asks.

Lo looks down at the floor, twiddles his thumbs. "We're being kinder to each other."

Her eyes shift to Jeremy.

"Yes, Davina, I think we've turned a corner."

Her smile beckons, asking us to join in her mirth. "Good, you two are each other's soulmates, like it or not. Very rare to find. Our soulmate challenges us, so it's not always easy to be with them. But you must persevere, you must. No one will love you like the other."

"But come, child," she says, dancing over. "We work best before the sun rises, so we must not waste any time." She gestures to a table with food. "Boys, you are welcome to my desserts, freshly baked."

Jeremy and Lo rub their hands together and begin to gorge.

Davina takes my hand, hers brittle, and we go into a room decorated by candles. There are two pillows on the ground, and she sits cross-legged on one, instructs me to do the same.

"Now, child, why have you come?"

I stare into her face. Her eyes so wide, expressive, and a deep-sea blue.

"I'm lost," I mumble. I tell her about Evan, and Love, about my failings as a mom. I tell her about fame and how it left me unfulfilled. About my neglecting parents and my dead sister. How I'm not even twenty-one years old and that I feel like I lived a thousand lives.

"You probably have," she says. "We all have. That's why we sleep so much every night. Our bodies need to recover from past traumas."

"What about present traumas?"

"Even more exhausting because we're still processing them."

"I am being watched."

I look around, just the moon winking outside of the window. But what of my shadow? Are they winking in secret too?

"Yes," she says, nodding like a bobblehead. "You are."

My mouth goes wide. "You can see this?"

"I can see a lot. Not with my eyes. With my soul."

"What does it see?"

She holds her hands, palms faced out. She sucks at the back of her teeth. I feel an energy transference. Crazy to say, but she's taking away a part of me, the sensation of it seeping out of my pores.

"When was the first time you saw this watcher?"

I tell her of the cabin and the shadow stalking. How I ran in fright, and it banged on my car as I sped away.

"No, there was a time before."

I flip back through my mind but can't think of what she means.

"Locate it," she orders. "Dig through cobwebs. You may have kept it hidden for a reason."

I swim through darkness, hoping for a spark of light in the deep recesses of my brain, but come up empty.

"Wait," she snaps. "Let me try."

Her palm on my forehead, so warm now it's almost hot. Her eyes roll to her skull, only whites staring back.

"You were singing at a show," she says, in an altered voice. "The show has ended, and you go back to your dressing room. A security guard is normally posted outside, but this security guard left for a moment, a tiny fraction of a second..."

A flash of this memory. I'm bathed in glitter, sweating from a set, having just played a local show in L.A., one of our last as Evanico. The crowd a beautiful roar that night, Evan and I in tune with one another. He was in his dressing room and I'm in mine, changing my top, when the door creaks open. I yell at what I think is the security guard, a teddy bear named Roy, but a different body enters. Well, more like crept inside— slithered. Skinny, skinny body, pale, pale skin, hollow eyes ringed with purple circles like he never sleeps, mostly bald with a comb-over and a few long hairs pasted down across his dome. His lips say my name and I shudder.

"What are you doing—?" I ask, covering myself up.

He locks the door behind him, coughs into his fist.

"I wanted to meet you," he says, his voice so high he sounds like a little girl.

"This is my private dressing room," I say, as if he doesn't already know.

"I wanted us to be alone."

I scream, guttural, from the depths. There's music playing outside, I think it's the Red Hot Chili Peppers' "Soul to Squeeze" over the sound system. No one can hear me.

He steps closer, cautiously. He has a limp. He's bruised. Beaten. Looking like he could crumble at any moment, yet I've never been more afraid of someone before. I taste death on my tongue, its iron tang.

"I just want to hold you," he says, breaking down. Tears zigzagging his cheeks. Body trembling. A lost puppy in a kennel.

"Don't come any closer."

I take a stand, my fists raised. I will beat this man. I will make sure he does not hurt me.

"But I need you," he cries. "Your songs. You are an angel."

"GET OUT!"

He comes at me, claws at my body, his hands slick like rain. He holds me for the worst seconds of my life before I barrel into him, knocking him to the ground. He's curled in a fetal position, moaning, as I race to the door, somehow get the lock open, and burst to my freedom. No one is outside, not Evan, not Roy, and I take off. I have a joint in my pocket and I smoke it to chill my nerves. I find a bar and drown the entire night in whiskey until what happened doesn't exist anymore, until I've forgotten it entirely.

And that's where it stayed, hidden where secrets fester, the ones that can poison you from within.

"Nico," I hear, and I'm brought back to Davina. She's whistling, a siren's song. I break through and hug her tight.

"Yes, yes, he tried to attack me. I was so scared, so scared."

I'm weeping on her blessed shoulder. She's running her fingers through my hair, attempting to soothe.

"He must be the shadow," I yell. "He's still after me."

Davina untangles from my embrace. "Possibly."

She starts blowing out the candles. The sun rising, the room aglow.

"I must have blocked it out," I say, and she nods.

"It is real," she says, ominously.

"But if he's my shadow, what can I do?"

She shrugs. "Whatever will happen has already happened. That is how time works. We think we exist in a linear fashion, but we do not."

I'm shivering, I'm so cold. The drum circle still pounds out by the beach, louder than before, like a jackhammer.

"Then it's hopeless."

I collapse into a ball of mush.

"No, no, child," she coos. "Nothing is hopeless. You have seen the face of your enemy, yes?"

"I guess."

"Then you know what to do when you see that face again."

"What?"

"I am not here to tell you that, only help you search for parts of yourself you have lost. But you are aware now, yes."

I manage to nod.

"Then you have the upper hand, no?"

"But you said whatever will happen has already happened?"

"Doesn't mean that you are not victorious...someday. Whenever that day is meant to be."

She yawns. "Now, you must go, child. You have drained me. I am a vampire. I sleep during the day."

She recedes into the shadows, maybe even vanishes. I gather myself and leave. In the other room, Jeremy and Lo are sleeping, wrapped up in each other, their stomachs fat and full. They look so peaceful I don't want to disturb them.

I kiss Jeremy on his beautiful cheek, my true savior. But I must go. Where I do not know, but not here, far away, where I can begin again.

Outside, the sun hits me like a slap across the face, coating me in lava. I walk all the way back to my car, and just drive. Drive until it's night. I don't know where I am, but I'm somewhere. I'm alive, I can feel it. I can feel myself pulsating.

26

• • • • •

WHERE ARE YOU NOW? – EVANICO

I can't believe my mom has identified her stalker! This creepy man who snuck into her dressing room has to have something to do with her disappearance. As I contemplate this, 9021-*Hole* checks into a motel overlooking the tail end of the beach, all sharing one room off my dad's credit card to save money. Each of us touch base at home, tells our parents we're fine.

I'm in the bathroom with the shower running now, sitting on the porcelain throne completely invested in my mom's journal. According to this good witch Davina, my mom wasn't crazy. There really was someone hunting her. I get chills imagining how she must've felt. It's the first time I want to read another entry right away, but there's a pounding knock on the door. Frankie.

"Hey, save some water for the dolphins," she shouts.

We hadn't really talked since we had our fight, avoiding one another while the tension reigned supreme.

I shut off the shower and open the door a crack. She

has her arms crossed.

"Caden's got to go."

I peer over at Caden, who's doing a pee pee dance.

"Sorry," I say, leaving the bathroom with the journal close to my chest as Caden darts in and slams the door.

Delilah's over by the mirror fixing her eye shadow. I can't believe the two of us kissed. I replay the feeling again and again in my brain. How soft her lips were. I'm unsure how much I liked it because she was a girl, or that I'd just never been kissed like that before. By anyone!

"There's a karaoke place down the block," Delilah says. "Not sure what else there is to do in a surfing town at night. Maybe your mom's there, since she's a singer?"

"Yeah, I saw it as well," Frankie says, in a pissy tone. "I was gonna suggest that too."

Eye brush in hand, Delilah rolls her eyes. "Were you?"

Frankie looks like she wants to murder the girl. "Yeah, I was."

"All right, it's settled then," I say, wanting to keep the peace.

Caden comes out of the bathroom wiping his forehead. "Phew, that was intense."

"We're going to karaoke," I say, and he shrugs.

The karaoke bar is filled with dudes and surfer chicks, all of them perfectly tanned, scattered sand on the floor. A guy up front is ruining "Don't Stop Believin'", a song I feel like everyone tries to sing in karaoke. A gaggle of girls are swooning in front of him, and he's getting bolder. We get a table in the back.

A waitress comes over and we order mocktails. I get a Shirley Temple, which is my favorite, sweet as hell with a maraschino cherry on top.

"So, how's the songwriting been going?" Frankie asks, elbowing me on my shoulder.

She's bringing this up because she's still miffed that I've never told her about this. And honestly, it wasn't ever something I made *that* big a deal about. I tried it out a few times to see if I could. And I'm not that good at all. In fact, I think I pretty much suck. But maybe it's one of the ways I can feel closer to my mom. Like maybe she was somewhere songwriting as well, the two of us tapping from the same kind of creative pool.

"I thought we tell each other *everything*," Frankie says, downing her mocktail like it's a shot. "Another," she barks, to the waitress.

I lick my lips, which still buzz from the kiss I just had with Delilah. I never keep major things from Frankie, but I don't want her judgmental reaction. Do I like girls? That'd be the first question out of her mouth, and I don't really know the answer...yet. I'd like to try it again, that I know.

"Whatever," Frankie says, making a W with her hands. The waitress brings her another drink and she focuses on sucking it down.

"Are you gonna sing?" Caden asks me, hiding behind his floppy hair.

"Are you?"

His eyes bug and he shakes his head, terrified.

Delilah pounds her fist on the table. "Well, I am." She marches up to the stage as the dude's "Don't

Stop Believin'" draws to a close. She grabs the mic from him, catching him off guard.

"This is for a new friend of mine," she says, giving the small crowd a wink and then launches into Katy Perry's "I Kissed a Girl (And I Liked It). The whole time she's gazing right at me. Everyone can see it. Frankie and Caden, their mouths dropped open. Delilah's got a soulful voice, not a surprise, putting real emotion into the song, bowing and weaving to the beat. The crowd eats her up, loving it all. They're looking at me too, like I'm her inspiration. I sip my Shirley Temple wanting to die, but knowing I have to maintain my cool. I have to act like this is perfectly normal and I'm not so embarrassed I want to melt into a puddle and slide down the drain. Besides, no one's ever sung like this to me before. No one's ever paid attention. And now Delilah seems like she cares about one person and one person only and that's me. She comes closer as she reaches the end of the song, our gazes locked. When she finishes, she tosses the mic over her shoulder and sits down like it's no big deal at all.

"What the—?" Frankie asks, her eyes like a tennis match batting back and forth between me and Delilah.

I can't look at her. I don't even know how to answer. Delilah's laughing, having the best time. A surfer girl hops over to congratulate her, she eyes me too with a smile. I can feel Frankie's gaze like a laser beam, penetrating. Since I'm not ready to respond, I jump up and head to the stage.

"She's singing?" I hear Caden gulp.

Yes, she's singing, I wanna say. *She's* doing a lot of things on this trip she never thought she would've done before. My mom had a life-changing experience years ago on her trip, and right now, I'm just like her.

I know what I have to sing.

I find it in the song book and key it up. "Where Are You Now?" by Evanico, the last single they released. Not a blockbuster hit like some of their others, but a quiet hit, the lyrics about a relationship that's run its course, each person wondering where their loved one has gone, what are they doing now? Apropos, right?

It also takes my mind off what just happened with Delilah. I'm still reeling from what I learned about my mom discovering who her stalker might be. But it doesn't seem right, a little too pat. If my mom was being followed by some crazed fan, she would've told my dad at the time, since they were still getting along during that first instance, or at least reported it to the police. Maybe that guy is just a red herring, and the real stalker was still clueless to her?

I'm singing and thinking all of this. I don't have a great voice. It's not like a cat's screech, no one's ears are bleeding, but there's no A&R guy in the audience like with my mom popping up to give me recording contract. Some of the surfer dudes are swaying. A golden tan in the front knows most of the words and sings along. Delilah's clapping in the back, and Frankie's got her arms crossed. I see her whisper something in Caden's ear and leave, barreling out of the karaoke bar. Who cares? She's not the center of attention anymore and it's eating her alive. Once she's gone, I'm able to feel the song better, less distracted. I'm singing my little heart out. Singing for mom as if she can hear and let me know where she's gone. End this broken record that's become my life.

When I finish, I'm teary-eyed and people are politely clapping. Delilah greets me with a big hug and a kiss on my cheek. The crowd whoops at that and I blush. The girl up front heads on the stage and starts singing "Surfin' U.S.A." like a joke.

Caden's eyes are on the door. "Should we go find her?" he asks.

I don't want to. Delilah shakes her head and it's decided.

I order another Shirley Temple, enjoying the sugar high and the natural high from this moment. Where all eyes were on me for once, and how Frankie just couldn't handle.

27

· · · · ·

ROAM – THE B-52s

Sometime in 1999

I decided to leave the United States, taking the money I earned from Evanico's album and flying to Europe. Since I never went to college, this would be my "study abroad". I was really out of other options. Staying in the States meant the possibility of my stalker finding me. I imagined myself returning back to Eugene and endangering Love and Evan. I don't know what I would do if I was the cause of something terrible happening to her.

I'd been chasing freedom this whole time. Nothing would be more freeing than wandering around Europe, so I bought a one-way ticket, beginning in Spain and heading east. I stayed in hostels, sometimes on benches. I had a backpack with a few clothes I would wash every couple of days in laundromats. I lived off *pan con tomate* and *gazpacho* in Barcelona and Madrid. I dyed my hair blonde and cut it super short, pixie like Mia Farrow in *Rosemary's Baby*, so no would recognize me. We had toured in Europe and hit the charts there. I met a student named Leon and we went skinny dipping in Barceloneta. He fell in love with me after two nights of just kissing, but I had to break his heart.

I went to France next, gorging myself with the cuisine. I ate so much I was no longer thin, but I didn't care. At no point did I see my stalker, and I wondered if I might be cured. That leaving the country was what kept me safe. In Paris, I linked up with a trio of Australian travelers. They rented a van and we drove down to the Riviera. We drank wine and ate baguettes with butter and brie cheese. One of them, Michael, had a guitar and he would play on the top of his van under the stars at night. I sang along to a version of The B-52s' "Roam", and they told me I had an amazing voice. I said no one had ever complimented me before. They suggested I make singing a career, and I laughed. I was so far from wanting it to be my career anymore, I couldn't imagine ever going up on stage again.

They drove me to Germany where we parted ways. I went to where the Berlin Wall used to stand, amazed that it had been just ten years since its fall. The murals painted in its place were beautiful and I cried for all the people who lived in East Germany before and how stuck they were. Hopeless.

From Germany, I went down into Switzerland, ate too much chocolate and fondue, before I went to Italy where I stayed for a long time. I gave up watches, calendars. I roamed, like The B-52s sang. From Northern

Italy in Piza, Genoa, Florence and Venice, down into Rome and Perugia and the Amalfi Coast to Naples. I consumed enough pasta to turn to wheat. I befriended an old woman who fed pigeons and let me stay in her empty bedroom. She listened to opera records really loud because she was practically deaf. The room was mostly barren. A thin bed and a box window that looked out on a courtyard. In the mornings, it smelled of fresh bread. She called me her *bambini* and I called her *mamma*. It made me miss my own parents and I'd cry some nights about how bad our relationship had become. I could call anytime, but too much time had passed. They had moved on and I could feel their distance. They didn't even know I'd left America, not sure when I'd ever return.

I didn't party in that small town where I stayed for many months. I wanted to be good. I wanted to reflect. I thought a lot about my past and how much had changed in the last few years. From being sixteen and insecure and never singing in front of a crowd to losing my sister and finding Grenade Bouquets. I'd messed up my relationship with all of them, my high school friends Jeremy and Winter too. It had been months since I'd been in touch with anyone, all of them forgetting about my presence.

When we were a band for that short amount of time, Grenade Bouquets felt like it ruled the world. Once we got Clarissa out of the picture. Ha! I remembered how shady I'd been in turning the band against her. I'm sure she still hates me, using my face as a dartboard. She never found success in another band, and that must have eaten her up. None of them did, except me and Evan. Randy and Ed tried to find other groups, but they mostly played local shows. Same with Lacey. She never managed anyone big. I believe she went back to college to earn her degree, but she was upset with me about how I handled the Clarissa situation. After the two of them became an item, she wanted nothing to do with me. The only one who put up with my nonsense was Evan, and even he'd given up now.

I picture myself returning home and how that would be. Love must be about a year and a half, forming words now, but not "mama". "Mama" doesn't exist. Even if I went back, he'd never let me really be a part of her life, too scared I'd run away again because that's what I do. I run away when things get hard. I did it when I was sixteen and I'm doing it for a third time now at twenty. I'm no longer a teen but I'm still acting like one. I don't know how to change. Returning home means my stalker could come back. I just know it. He's creepily waiting for me to get close, so he can attack. I can't chance it. I must continue to roam. But at least I don't feel crazy anymore. I'm returning more to who I used to be, when I was sane. This tiny room in this very small town of a few hundred people and this old woman who listens to opera so loud have been my saviors. They've resurrected me, and I'll forever be grateful.

One day I'll leave. I'm sure of it. I'll find the *cojones* to return home. To my daughter, to my reality. But not yet. I'm not ready. I need to vanish just a little longer. I'll be in touch, some day, I promise. But for now, I'm gone.

28

• • • • •

IN THE FOREST – SCREAMING TREES

We're in Muir Woods where my mom got arrested almost two decades ago. She'd been protesting deforestation and had chained herself to a tree. This was right before she met Dad. After that stop, she'd go to Eugene, sing Tori Amos' "Silent All These Years" at an Open Mic sesh at Café Hey and capture his attention. I'd just read my mom's last journal entry—her jaunt to Europe in an attempt to be free. Grenade Bouquets and its members had been on her mind then. How the band hit such great heights and then imploded.

I'd heard a little about the band from my dad. All of them except my mom met as freshmen at the University of Oregon. Well, not their drummer Randy because he was like thirty at the time. Lacey was their manager; Ed was the party animal who played bass. And Clarissa was the lead singer and my dad's ex. He said they had a pretty awful relationship. She was moody and difficult and prone to cheating on him. He kept going back to her until he finally gave up, then he met my mom who worked her magic to get Clarissa out of the band. It was after that that their song "Ready to Guide" blew up. Clarissa had never been a part of their success.

The drive up from Pismo Beach had been less than stellar. Tension filled the air. Frankie was still mad at me, and I could see her in the backseat giving sour looks my way in the rearview. Caden, of course, took her side and fawned all over her, making her feel special. Delilah sat shotgun. It was kind of weird between us after our kiss and she sang to me at karaoke. We hadn't had a chance to be alone yet to talk, so she just fiddled with the radio, settling on a hard rock station playing Screaming Trees "In the Forest" as we pulled up to Muir Woods.

My God, Muir Woods was beautiful. Giant redwood trees, the air so clean if felt refreshing to breathe (especially after the smogfest of L.A.). Frankie and Caden went off on their own, and I wasn't ready to have a major convo with Delilah about what we were to one another, so I said I needed to call my dad.

In truth, I do need to call him so I can get info about the rest of his band. There's so many pages of heavy writing left in Mom's journal, I can't imagine her stalker situation was solved. Something seems too easy about the man in her dressing room being the one. I could feel that in my gut. I wonder if her old bandmates might've played a bigger part, since it ended so poorly between them all.

"Hey, Love," my dad says, so excited to hear my voice. It makes me realize how lucky I am to have at least one great parent.

"Hey, Dad, we're in Muir Woods."

"Ah, the place of your mom's brush with the law."

"Haha, yeah, I guess."

"I really don't think she'd want to return to that scene of the crime."

"You're probably right, I dunno. Yeah, this whole going to old haunts of hers doesn't seem to be working." I lean against a large tree that twists up into the sky and slide down to the earth. "I was wondering about Grenade Bouquets?"

His voice gets cold and prickly. "What do you want to know about it?"

"Like, have you been in touch with any of the other members since?"

He blows out a long breath. "Not...really. Things got bad between us all. They blamed your mom for getting the attention and I took her side. Then they blamed me for us breaking up."

"That's ridiculous."

"I know. Ya-know, it was jealousy really. Your mom had the spotlight. There was no room for anyone else's egos."

"So, you haven't spoken—"

"These days it's easier to know what someone's up to as opposed to back then. Ed, lemme see, last I heard he was in Portland. He owns a bar I think, like a biker bar. And Randy, he got married and adopted a few children. I think he lives in the Caribbean, or...I'm not sure, somewhere outside of the States where gay marriage is legal. And Lacey, she was managing this small band somewhere in the Pacific Northwest. The Retrofitters, something like that. I think she's married with a kid as well. We all grew up."

"And Clarissa?"

He gets silent.

"Yeah, we haven't been in touch at all," he finally says. "She had a really hard time with your mom becoming lead singer. I know she tried to find other bands, but between the two of us, she wasn't too talented a singer. She wanted it, though, so I'm sure that was a tough pill to swallow."

"Do you think she ever got over it?"

"I can't say. I would hope so. It's been almost two decades, so if she's still simmering with resentment, well, that's just no good. Even after all that happened between us, I wish her the best."

Delilah walks over. She's in a cool checkered coat, wearing stockings with runs, her lipstick so red it hurts to look at.

"I should go, Dad."

"Okay, Love, you stay safe, and I'll see you soon."

"Miss you," I say, the words leaving my mouth unawares.

"Oh, well, I miss you too. Always, honey. Thanks for checking in. I'm really so proud of how adult you've become."

"Bye, Dad." I hang up, my heart swelling. I really do miss him. This is the longest we've ever spent apart.

"How's the old man?" Delilah asks.

"He's good. I was asking about my mom's band. I'm wondering if one of them might've been her stalker?"

Delilah kicks a rock. "You think?" She whips out her phone. "Let's *stalk* them and see."

I respond with a smile. While I'm against Smartphones and the way they're controlling the world, this time I'll let it slide.

Within a few minutes, she has all of their info on display.

Every one of them easily able to find.

Everyone except Clarissa.

29

• • • • •

WHERE IS MY MIND? – THE PIXIES

Fall 1999

Coming back to America is bittersweet. I will miss my elderly roommate and all the opera records she would play. The pigeons mating by my window in the palazzo. I will not miss the twenty pounds I gained from Italy's wonderous food, but that's really the least of my worries. It was time for me to return home. I couldn't avoid Evan and Love forever. I couldn't live with myself if I did. And I had to face my other fear: whether or not the shadow who followed me was still a threat. I needed to confront him head-on if I was ever going to fully heal.

In Europe, I lost the taste for drugs and drink. I meditated every day. I didn't check the *Billboard* charts. I'd attained what I wanted more than anything—freedom.

Showing up at Evan's door and knocking was the hardest thing I'd ever done. I stopped myself a few times, almost chickened out, before I took a chance.

Trembling, I knocked and when he opened the door, I practically puked on the floor.

"Nico?" he asked, blinking as if I was a ghost.

He didn't welcome me in right away, kept me at a distance. Even once I was sitting on the couch, he hovered in the kitchen like I was nuclear. I'd catch him staring in disbelief. He never thought he'd see me again.

"Can I see her?" I asked, tears in my throat.

He shook his head. "I have to think about that. Give me time."

I gave him the time he needed. I rented a condo apartment a mile down the road from him. I never showed up uninvited. He would stop by to check on me—Love in the car seat. I'd stand on my tiptoes at the door just to see a glimpse of her. It was always during her naptime. He beckoned one day for me to come outside. He'd gotten scruffier. His blond beard taking over the rest of his face. His kind blue eyes almost hidden. I peered through the window and watched her sleep. She had such fine blond hair, like him, sitting on the top of her tiny head like fine pulls of cotton candy.

I looked up in his eyes, mine brimming with tears. I longed to hold her, but he wasn't ready. He didn't want to give her any kind of false hope. I understood.

So, we continued this dance. He'd come back and slowly, slowly let me get closer to Love. He brought her inside one day. Clutching her little hand as she hid behind his leg.

"Don't be scared," I said, offering a lollypop. "It's okay."

She cried, a loud scream. Her cheeks so red. She wanted nothing to do with me. I couldn't blame her.

"Give her time," Evan said.

I got a job at Café Hey as a barista. I learned to make coffee and decorate with foam designs. I wasn't great, but people in town were fascinated. I was *that singer* (!). *What was I doing here??*

"I'm taking some time for myself," I'd say, and then choke on the last words. "For my family…"

Sometimes Evan would get a babysitter and play a set at Open Mic. He'd do covers: Beck's "Loser", Garbage's "Only Happy When It Rains", Weezer's "Say It Ain't So", and my favorite, The Pixies' "Where Is My Mind?" Part of me wanted to jump on that stage and sing with him, but the consequences were too great. I'd been good with my addiction, *all* of my addictions: my shadow stalker included. I didn't want to let singing and the spotlight cause me to slip.

We had a weekly family dinner on Sunday nights. I would cook, or at least attempt to cook. Love started coming around. She'd call me Nico, never mom because that would be too cruel to do. And Evan and I formed a newfound friendship. We were kind to one another, not judgmental. He didn't ream me out for my past mistakes. He congratulated me for how far I'd come.

I'd even gotten in touch with my parents again. Nothing crazy, just a phone call here and there. Mom was enjoying being a newlywed with Roger Ferguson. They honeymooned in Bora Bora. And Dad was Dad—busy with work, laser-focused on money. Although Annette seemed to be helping him take the occasional day off here and there.

I got back in touch with Winter and Jeremy too. Winter had her baby, Delilah, and we swore we'd introduce our offspring to each other soon. Jeremy had fully moved in with his boyfriend Lo and it seemed like it was getting super serious. They both appeared to be good, older, but so was I.

And then, tragedy. Well. What did I expect? I was coming home from Café Hey one night and, in the distance, saw my shadow lurking. I dropped my keys to the ground and had to hunt around in the mud to find them, my heart slamming into my chest, a metal taste of fear in my mouth. The shadow came closer. It was a full moon night, so I was able to see them more clearly than ever before. They wore a cap, their face darkened, but I spied long hair on them this time. And their body was different than how I remembered. Not a man's body, but breasts! A woman after me. Had it been a woman all along, and I'd failed to notice?

I finally found my keys, thrust them in the lock, and bolted inside.

This kept happening, again and again, this shadow outside my door late at night. I had to quit my job at Café Hey. I became a shut-in. I'd spend my days watching through the blinds for a hint of their presence. I stopped sleeping. I turned to alcohol again. Just a sip here and there and then so much more. Days passing that I couldn't recall.

I tried to keep this from Evan, but it was futile. He could smell my descent on my breath. My poison. He was embarrassed. Frustrated. Disappointed. He wouldn't let me near Love if I stayed like this. I tried to tell him about my shadow. That it could be a woman, not this man who'd broken into my dressing room years ago. I'd never told him about what happened, and so he didn't believe me. He wanted me to go back to the clinic in town. But they never helped me. They didn't believe me. I was trapped. I needed to be free again. The only place I could be free was back in Italy in that old lady's boarding room with opera crackling through the walls and the pigeons cooing outside. My shadow never found me there. My mind at peace. It was lost now, and I needed to find it again.

I left. No horrible note this time. Just my departure. I cried the whole flight there with Love's face burning in my vision. As moms go, I was the worst. A complete and utter failure, but I needed to leave to survive. If I stayed, I feared I'd vanish in a different way: a permanent end to my existence.

So, I had no choice. I told myself this over and over.

I had no choice.

I had no choice.

Right?

30

· · · · ·

STUPID GIRL – GARBAGE

Delilah does some digging on her phone and magically she gets the numbers for Ed, Randy, and Lacey. Randy's on Facebook, Ed has a homepage offering music lessons, and Lacey's a manager courting clients. No info on Clarissa yet, but this is a good start. Since Frankie and Caden haven't returned from wandering off, we might as well give this a try before they do and cause havoc. I know Frankie will want to talk about what's happened between us on this trip. If I really thought about it, we were starting to become more distant from one another. Maybe she realized I had feelings about her, and it got awkward, or maybe I was trying not to confront how I felt so I'd been more aloof. Still, it was there—this gap between us. And until we talked, it would likely never be filled.

"What are you gonna say to them?" Delilah asks. We stare at a picture of Ed on his website: bald and pushing forty, listed as the "Best Bass Guitarist in the PNW".

"The truth," I say, as she presses the call button before I can change my mind.

"Yello, this is Ed." His voice gruff, like he'd been gargling alcohol.

"Hi. Ed, hi."

"Yes, hi, who is this?"

"You don't know me, but my name is Love. I'm Nico's daughter. Nico, who you used to—"

"Yeah, yeah, I know who she is. So, hi. Uh, what's this about?"

"My mom. Obviously. I know you haven't talked in a long time."

He laughs but it's not a happy laugh. "Not since I left the apartment we all had on the Lower East Side back in 1996."

"Right. Yeah, I know the band broke up. But, she's missing."

"Missing?"

Delilah gives a gesture for me to explain more.

"Vanished really. Over two months ago and no one's heard from her."

My voice shaking, my heart shaking. These people from her old life my last hope.

"Oh, I'm—yeah, I'm really sorry. But, I dunno, kid. I dunno where she would be."

"Right." I tip my head back as a cloud covers the sun. I'm cold. "Yeah, stupid, I guess. I don't know."

"Your mom, ya-know, I mean, she really pissed me off when we played together, but what raw talent. I've been in many, many bands and never came across pipes like hers. She marched to the beat of her own drum, though. Probably still doing that now."

"I'm sorry I called you."

"Nah, don't think nothing of it." I think I hear him burp. "Good luck with the search."

He clicks off. Randy's next. I take a deep breath and dial. Delilah's holding my hand this time.

"Hello?"

"Hi, Randy…" I give the same spiel I did to Ed.

"Oh no," he says. "Oh, that's just awful. How many months has she been gone? Two? I'm in the Caribbean. Moved shortly after the band imploded, so we've really been out of touch. Maybe Evan would know?"

"Yeah, he's my dad."

"Oh really? Oh Evan, yes, I have a flood of memories coming back. It's been so long."

"Can you think of anyone else who may have been in touch with her still?"

"Did you try Lacey? Those two were such good friends. I mean, until things got bad between us. But maybe her?"

"Okay."

"You tell Evan I said hi. Please tell him for me."

"I will."

"Please do. And if he wants to be in touch—"

"Whoops your call is dropping," I say, hanging up. Randy's the type to never shut up. Delilah makes a face.

"Last one," she says.

"This isn't working."

"Maybe she has info about Clarissa, since there's no web presence?"

"Okay, okay." I dial. A few rings pass. Finally, she picks up. The song "Stupid Girl" by Garbage faintly playing in the background.

"This is Lacey."

Her voice sweet, like I imagined. She'd been the one to first encourage my mom to sing. Lacey setting forward a chain of events that no one could ever foresee.

"Hi, Lacey..." And then my spiel again, almost out of breath when I finish.

"Wow, didn't expect that," Lacey says. I think I hear her lighting a cigarette and taking a puff. "Grenade Bouquets," she says, wistfully. "Like from another life."

"So, you haven't been in touch with her?"

"To be honest, your mom and I were really close, but she wasn't a good friend."

"I'm sorry."

"Not your fault, not hers either. We were so young. But I started dating Clarissa—I assume you know about Clarissa—and she wasn't supportive. We had a bad fight. That was one of the last times we spoke."

I hesitate, but Delilah squeezes my hand, encourages me to go on.

"Are you still in touch with Clarissa?"

She pauses while she takes a long drag. "Off and on."

I start jumping up and down, Delilah too. "Really?" I ask.

"We dated for a bit after the band felt apart."

"Do you have her info now?"

"Not her current phone number, sorry. A couple years back, we got back together. It was kinda a disaster. Here's a tip. Once you break up with someone, *stay* broken up. It never gets any better. Same problems always surface. She changed her number."

"Where was she living?"

"In Seattle. I assume she's still there. You ever heard of the Seattle freeze? That's Clarissa in a nutshell. Ice queen."

"What's her last name?" I ask, Delilah nodding for me to continue.

Lacey doesn't answer. I may have gone too far, probed too much. Finally, she lets out a deflated laugh.

"She's not gonna know anything about your mom."

I want to tell her that I believe they had unfinished business. That someone was stalking my mom and she realized it was a woman. That it could have been Clarissa.

"Bakenstock," Lacey finally says. "So, she's probably the only Clarissa Bakenstock."

"Bakenstock," I repeat out loud to Delilah, who starts searching on her phone.

"I really hope you find her. Your mom," Lacey says. "Even though it didn't all end well. She and I had some great times, and we were a part of something truly badass—this female fronted band with a female manager in the sexist 1990s. Seems crazy to think now, but we were one of the only ones. And Evanico, what she and your dad created. Some amazingly beautiful songs."

"Thank you, Lacey, for all your help."

She takes one last suck. I hear her grind out her cigarette in an ashtray.

"Yeah, well, it was nice to relive that past," she says. "Even for just a moment. You'll find your mom. She's a cockroach, and I mean that in the best way. She can survive anything."

She hangs up, having enough of that conversation.

"Clarissa's address," Delilah, showing me on the phone. She hugs me and plants a friendly kiss on my lips.

Over her shoulder, Frankie and Caden return, seeing everything.

31

• • • • •

BITTER SWEET SYMPHONY – THE VERVE

Frankie takes off, and I'm running after her like a fool. I'm not even thinking about Delilah or that quick kiss because I'm not sure I felt anything that time. I appreciate Delilah helping me with the search for my mom, but it wasn't like the movies, where my toes swelled, or my stomach dropped, and I swooned. That last kiss could've been anyone's lips.

Frankie's fast, so it's hard to keep up. I'm not actually athletic, so the gap between us widens. I yell her name, just in case she doesn't realize I'm trailing her, but she doesn't turn around. She goes even faster.

"Frankie, Frankie."

I'm crying now, the wind tearing against my face. Dodging looming trees. My legs splattered with mud. I don't care. I have no idea what I'll do when I catch up with her, only that the *need* to be with her is stronger than it's ever been. I want to kiss her. I know that now. I want to be with her always. No one makes me laugh like her or gets me out of my shell. She is superhuman.

"Frankie, stop, wait!"

My voice echoes through Muir Woods, bounces off the Redwoods. I get a burst of adrenaline, running faster than ever before until she's within reach. I try to grab, desperate, a twist of her shirt in my palm. I pull and we're on the ground.

"What the fuck?" she says, pushing me off her.

We're panting. I'm inhuman. She looks so pretty. A large flannel shirt like a dress. Her pale, pale legs. Doc Martins. Her new hairdo—combed with a barrette in the shape of a guitar by her ear.

"I'm sorry!" I say, tears spewing. "I'm sorry, Frankie."

She brushes mud off her shirt. "Sorry for what?"

"Sorry for—I don't know!"

These last few days of me and Frankie fighting have been the most untethered of my life. Even more than when I found out my mom vanished. Frankie *is* the closest person in my life.

"How can you be sorry if you don't know what you're sorry for?" she asks.

"Okay! For kissing Delilah. I'm sorry about that!"

Frankie stands. "I don't care if you kiss her."

"What?"

"I don't care who you kiss."

You, I long to say. I want to be kissing you.

"I do," I say, standing on shaky legs. We're so close, I *could* kiss her. All these years leading up to this moment.

"Love," she says, in a disappointing tone.

Don't break my heart, don't break my heart.

"I love you," I say, quickly, as if it can erase the

bomb she's about to drop.

"Love," she says again, more serious this time. "I have to tell you something."

"But I…"

She twists her sleeves around. "I'm different."

"What?"

"I'm…I'm just not interested in…" She swallows, her lip trembling. I want to hug her, my heart on fire.

"Me?"

I sound so small, a tiny mouse. I want to crawl into a hole and die.

"No, it's not…" She pinches the bridge of her nose. "I love you too. I really do."

"Really?"

"But not like that. Not like how you might want me to. And I've known this is how you felt for a while. I mean, I'd be dumb not to."

She takes a step back, never seeming so far away.

"Oh."

"But let me explain. I don't love anyone. I mean, this isn't easy. I don't really understand it myself, but like, sex, it doesn't interest me."

"What do you mean?"

"Like ever. Like, I dunno, obviously most everyone thinks about it *all* the time. I have never, really, like with a guy or girl, it doesn't matter. Kissing, anything like that, I just…I dunno, I don't know if I ever want to do it."

I put aside my battered feelings at the moment, process what she's saying.

"I don't understand."

"Asexual, I mean, that's the term I guess, although

who knows? I just know it's not something I'm interested in. Like at all. Ever. It's weird. Bodies are weird. And the thought of…" She shivers like she has goosebumps. "I'm sorry, Love. I know that's not what you want to hear."

I'm stunned, lovesick and spinning. I need to sit down.

"No. I'm sorry I… Why didn't you ever tell me?"

"Why didn't you ever tell me you liked me?"

She's smiling now. It allows me to mimic hers.

"Not easy to say, right?" she says. "I'm still figuring it out myself. What it means."

"Have you ever told anyone?"

"Yeah. Caden."

This hurts. It's like she stuck a dagger in my gut.

She sighs. "It's not my place to say more, that's for him to tell you. But he understands in a way that no one else can. So, we've talked about it a lot."

9021-*Hole* had never been a trio. It had always been the two of them with me as the third wheel.

"Are you okay?" she asks, and I don't know. I'm jumbled, that's for sure. "I love you, Love. You are my best friend in the whole wide world, and I want to know you for the rest of our lives. I really mean that."

"Why did you run away when you saw me and Delilah kiss?"

"It's weird for me, seeing that and knowing it'll never be something I wanna do. I'm still getting used to coming to terms with it."

"I can't believe I never knew," I say. "Like I was so wrapped up in myself I never noticed—"

"I hide it well. I mean, it's weird, or not weird

exactly, it's normal for me. Weird for everyone else."

"Yeah."

"Maybe you secretly loved me because you knew nothing could ever happen between us?" she says, shrugging her shoulders. "Maybe you and Delilah…?"

I think of Delilah, how magical that first kiss first. How the second one might've only been less because Frankie came back in the picture. And now that nothing would ever happen with Frankie, maybe…?

"Go for it," Frankie says. "And *I'm* sorry. I've been awful to you this trip. Here your mom went missing and I'm giving you crap about making a new friend. I was jealous of Delilah, not in a sexual way obviously, but because you and her got close so fast. I'm gonna lose you to someone someday, and I'm starting to realize that."

"No! Frankie, we'll always be close—"

"You'll fall in love. It's cool. I'll be happy for you when you do."

She's tearing, I'm bawling. We hug and I feel safe again. I don't want to let go.

"Promise from now on that we don't keep secrets from each other?" I say.

She holds out her pinkie. "Pinkie swear."

We walk back to the car, holding hands as friends. I feel strangely settled, like I'm glad at the outcome, like the pressure between us is gone. Delilah's laying on the hood wearing headphones. She props herself on her elbow and winks at me. I do want to get to know her better, see if there could be something between us, if I'm meant to date girls.

"You all okay?" Delilah asks, taking off her headphones. "Bitter Sweet Symphony" by The Verve blares. This whole trip has been a bittersweet symphony: some bad mixed with the good. I guess that's life.

The last part of the trip would be to find Clarissa in Seattle, get some final answers. But Eugene is on the way there. I miss my dad. I miss my bed. I'm tired. So, it's time to go home.

We get in the car, and I drive out of Muir Woods. Everyone can feel it, like our journey is over. In the backseat, Caden leans on Frankie's shoulder. Silent Caden. I'm glad he has Frankie to open up to. I can't be mad about that. She gives me a wave through the rearview, her eyes tossing at Delilah, telling me to go for it. Delilah's got her feet propped up, her hand close to mine. With my left hand on the wheel, I inch my right one toward her, our fingers touching. And then we hold. She doesn't break away. We stay linked for the rest of the trip until we get back to Oregon.

Until I come home.

32

• • • • •

FOUND OUT ABOUT YOU – GIN BLOSSOMS

December 31, 1999

I celebrate the end of the century in a tiny bedroom in Italy. I have party favors and watch it on a small television with an antenna. I've been back here for months now. This is my home. I haven't seen my stalker. Not a peep. I've never been crazy, just unfortunate. And my stalker knows me, she has to. Back when I was staying in Eugene, she followed my work schedule, stood in the right place outside of my window, so she still could be hidden by the shadows. But her long hair gave her away. I've only made one enemy in life and that's Clarissa. She'd want revenge and what better revenge could there be to make me feel like I'm losing my mind. I took Evan and Grenade Bouquets from her, now she'd steal my sanity.

Long after the ball dropped, I'm listening to Gin Blossoms' "Found Out About You", singing louder than I have sung in a long time. The walls are thin, and the entire building can hear my triumph. Whenever I'm ready to return to the States, I will find her, I will hunt her, I will make sure she does not cause me pain anymore. I will get back to Love and be normal. I will write songs and perform, maybe not for the masses, but for small crowds. Evan and I could become friends again, maybe never lovers, but that's okay. We can respect one another and that will be enough. I'll form new relationships with my parents that are healthy. I'll keep Winter and Jeremy closer in my life. I won't touch alcohol or drugs. Or even better, get to a place where I can have an occasional sip or toke but not rely on it. I'll treat my body kindly. I'll be a role models for girls. This fantasy is in reach. It doesn't have to be a fantasy. But for me to return, Clarissa needs to go away. And I don't know if I'm ready for that yet.

This tiny bedroom has become a sanctuary. I can be anyone here, warts and all. Through the door and on a plane is a different story. And one day, I'll take that leap. A New Year's promise.

If I swear to this, I have to make it come true.

I fall asleep more hopeful than ever. I have Candy Land dreams of sugarplum fairies. Everything bathed in gold. I'm flying, I'm soaring, I don't need to look down. There are no clouds, just an amazing sun, its warmth soothing. I'm flying so close I can almost touch it, the heat like a red-hot breath on my skin, hotter, hotter, my fingertips searing, and I'm ablaze, a phoenix, rising, tangled in flames, reborn.

33

• • • • •

TONES OF HOME – BLIND MELON

Back in Eugene, I drive my travel-mates home one-by-one. Caden is first, and I park my car and walk him up to the door to say a proper goodbye. It took this trip to realize that we never spent any time alone, and that would change. He's a good friend, and I had to stop taking him for granted.

He picks at his eyebrow ring, his bangs cover the top half of his eyes.

"I wanted to thank you," I say, as he has his hand on the doorknob.

He shrugs his thin shoulders. "For what?"

"Dropping everything to come with me on this insane road trip."

He kicks at a patch of dirt, never looks me in my eyes. "Not like I had that much to drop."

"Yeah, tell me about it." I step closer to him and can feel his nervous energy. "But really, thank you. You mean a lot to me, Caden."

His eyes bug, dumbfounded that I'd even notice

his presence.

"I don't have a lot of friends, but you're one of my best, you and Frankie."

He pulls at his sleeves. "Yeah. You, too."

"And you can tell me anything, ya-know. We never just hang out, you and I. That should change."

His cheeks turn red. "I-I'd like that."

Someday, I'd hope he'd feel comfortable enough to open up to me. Frankie had said that he understood her more than anyone else could, so I wonder if he's the same as her? But it's not my business to pry. Only if he's ready to tell me more.

I give him a big dwarfing hug, his bones so soft, like I could crush him. But he hugs me back.

"Say hi to your moms for me," I say.

He's about to open the door when he asks: "Maybe we can have you over for dinner sometime? They make a mean veggie lasagna."

I really would like to talk to his moms more, about these new feelings I have, even about Delilah. It's like he senses this.

"That would be great."

"Bye, Love."

"Bye," I say, but he's already disappeared inside.

Frankie's next. We're playing Blind Melon's "Tones of Home" when we pull up to her house. Her mom sits on her porch in a house dress and gives a giant wave. She looks good. Better than she's looked in some time.

"Oh jeez," Frankie says. "The welcoming party is already out in full force."

"Say hi to Shelia for me," I say.

Frankie puts on her backpack. "So, folks, it's been

wild," she says, with a shaka sign.

"It was good to meet you," Delilah says to her nails.

Frankie bows her hands in prayer. "Nah, I was a gnarly wench to you, but I'm sorry."

Delilah looks up from her painted nails. "Apology accepted."

"You got a pretty amazing human there," she says, nodding at me. "And I'm fiercely protective, so treat her right."

Delilah smiles in my direction. "You can count on it."

Frankie steps out of the car. "Later skaters."

As she's walking up to her house, I bolt out of the car and give her a strangling hug from behind.

"I love you," I whisper in her ear. "Best friend."

She reaches back to hug. "Best friend." She spins around. "And let me know what happens with your mom's frenemy, Clarissa. Whether or not she was her stalker."

"I will."

"Tootles," Frankie says, and kisses me on the cheek.

"Hi, Love," Frankie's mom calls out, and I wave back. I watch them hug, Frankie's mom bathing her in kisses. My stomach gets squishy. Would my mom ever do that to me again? Had she ever? I need to look away.

I get back into my car and Delilah's still singing along to Blind Melon.

"So, I think I'm gonna stay at my Gram's," she says. "I talked to my mom, and we realized it would be good for us to have a break from one another."

"Really? You just called her now?"

"I'd been working on it for some time. Gram Edina

has always wanted me to spend more time with her. Maybe you could visit, or I can come back up here?"

I wrinkle my nose, so pumped. "That'll be awesome."

"Well, after you finish the hunt for Nico Sullivan of course."

"Of course."

"Where can I take you?" I ask.

"Airport, Winter says it's on her dime."

When I drop Delilah off, I'm giddy, because it's not saying goodbye but see you soon. As planes take off around us, she leans in for a kiss, and I let her. It doesn't curl my toes like the first time, or is quick like the second, just sweet. I don't know how long we kiss for, only that the world feels right and then I never want it to end.

"Give me a call when you get back from Seattle," she says, "and we'll make a plan."

"Okay." We're holding hands, not ready to let go. "You really...you've really helped me with so much," I say. "My mom, my feelings..." I'm not making any sense. I want to express how important she's been, but words don't seem to suffice. "I've never met anyone like you before."

She launches her head back with a booming laugh. She has such a great laugh. "I can honestly say I've never met anyone like you before, Love."

I do a ta-dah dance. "They broke the mold, I guess."

"They sure did."

We kiss again, and I don't care who's looking. I don't care about anyone else in this moment.

She pulls away. "Till next time."

"Always till next time."

I'm filled with gooey happiness for everyone, all this love I've seen and experienced. I carry it back home where my dad is mowing the front lawn. He's dirty and sweaty and I leap out of the car and nearly tackle him to the ground.

"Whoa, whoa," he says, as I hug his chest tight. He smells like he hasn't showered, but I don't care. He's the best dad in the world and I wouldn't trade him for anyone.

Arm-in-arm we head inside. I'm talking a mile-a-minute, telling him about my whole jaunt. The ups and the downs. Grandma Luanne's craziness, Grandpa Peter's health, how Great Aunt Carly predicted that things would change between me, Frankie, and Caden on the trip and how she was right. Seeing Jeremy and Winter. And meeting Winter's daughter Delilah who invited me back to visit sometime.

"Sure, we can arrange that this summer. Maybe I'd take an L.A. trip with you?"

"Dad," I say, not sure how I want to go about this. "There's another place I want to go to first."

I tell him about Mom's journals and everything I learned. How she really believed that someone was following her and how that someone could be Clarissa. How Delilah found her address. How I need to go to talk to her about Mom.

Dad gets these worry wrinkles on his forehead. "Love, I think you should maybe give this up."

"Give up Mom?"

"No. Well, yes. Somewhat." He goes to the fridge and grabs a beer, pops the tab. "She doesn't want to be found."

"How do you know?"

"Because this is what she does." He's raising his voice, then calms himself. "She leaves for some time, years even, and then dances back like nothing's happened. It's not fair to you."

"I can handle it," I say, thumping my chest. "I'm not some little girl. And I really believe she left for a reason out of her control. She *was* being watched and it scared her. She didn't want to put you and especially me in danger."

"But we weren't in danger."

"*She* believed we were. And if Clarissa had something to do with this... I only have a few more entries in her journal to finish. We can read them together. I can show you."

He brings the bottle to his forehead, dabs his sweat with its cool.

"I want to let you know that things between me and Marjorie are getting serious."

"Okay."

"I'm not ever getting back together with your mom."

He looks so sad, like he thinks he's shattering my heart with this info.

"Dad, I don't care about that. You two are terrible together. Trust me, I've read the blow by blows. And I like Marjorie. Really. I'll like whoever makes you happy, I don't care. But I really believe that Mom has been hurting for a long, long time and you and I are the only ones who could help bring her some closure. Maybe Clarissa can bring her this closure?"

"You just got back, and you want to travel again?"

"It's only Seattle. We can make the drive tomorrow.

It's the weekend, you don't have any summer classes."

"I'm not that excited to see Clarissa. You know things didn't end well between us."

"Please, please do this for me. I've never felt closer to Mom than on my trip, reading her journal, even the parts that were hard to hear. She loved Kurt Cobain. She ran away from home to meet him at his house. What if she's there now? What if she left me all these clues for me to go there? To find her. To allow her to apologize?"

I know he doesn't get a lot of what I'm saying, but he can't break my heart. He never could. He gives a quick nod, and I almost knock him over again with a hug.

"Okay, okay, Love. Okay."

"You are the best dad *ever*." I'm getting teary-eyed. "Seriously. I've always been upset that I didn't really have a mom growing up. But I did. It was you. You were my mom and my dad. And I love you."

"Oh, Love, I love you too."

We hug and then I pull away because I get a whiff of my pits.

"Woof," I say. "I'll need to pack an overnight bag with new clothes. Because these have become quite ripe."

I head to my bedroom. Throw my suitcase on my bed and lie down. I'm exhausted, but not tired, emotionally spent. I look around at my walls filled with grunge heroes. These idols, most of them long passed on, who my mom worshipped as well.

"I'm not the same girl I was when I left," I tell Cobain, Weiland, Cornell. Can they hear me in heaven? I tell Courtney Love here on Earth. I've played their music loud when I thought they were the only ones who could understand my pain. But I was wrong. I had an army. We might be the Ghosts to some back at school, but that didn't matter. To my true people, I was important. I mattered. Frankie. Caden. Dad. And now...Delilah.

I could still taste her kiss, a mixture of lipstick and strawberry Chapstick. I'll carry it with me tomorrow. Her presence holding my hand when we'd confront Clarissa and finally get some answers. And then, whether or not my mom's in Seattle waiting for me, I'd return home with the knowledge I'd done everything I could.

And that, would have to be enough.

I put Blind Melon's CD in my Aiwa boombox and crank "Tones of Home", singing to the sky, letting it give me the power I need for this last leg of my journey.

"And so, I wave goodbye, I'm flying, I'm fly-iiiiing."

34

· · · · ·

DEMONS – GUSTER

Spring 2000

I return to the States, not to see Love yet, but to confront my stalker. In some ways, I understand why she has tormented me. A few years ago, I stole her man and her band. Granted, she and Evan have broken up, but I still think she carried a torch. And Grenade Bouquets had been her dream. We got noticed when I attacked her on stage, but no one ever wrote about her. I was the star. She, a faded memory. When we gained traction, she wasn't mentioned at all, as if she never even existed. That would've pissed me off too.

Here I was: younger, hungrier. She didn't stand a chance. And we soared for a minute. That must've stung. But what had to have stung even more was when Evan and I had a child together and soared up the charts as Evanico. She never stalked me in Grenade Bouquets—what truly set her hair on fire was Evan and I finding success together, even though as a couple we're in tatters.

So, what will I do? I have found where she lives, moving to Seattle. This was not hard. I have mimicked what she has done, standing outside her apartment in the shadows like her. She has a roommate. They have a punk style, their hair in mohawks. She works in a gym at the front desk. She seems melancholy, going through the motions, hidden behind heavy eye shadows and lip liners. She cries mascara tears at night, I'm sure of it. Will she be honest about what she's done to me? How she's infected my life like a parasite? Will she apologize? I don't know what I want. If she stops—and this is hard to admit—I must face other fears. Have I been using her as a crutch? Made her into the sole reason responsible for my endless suffering? Will I have to grow up once she quits? Become the mom I need to be?

I'll confront her tomorrow outside of her gym. So she won't be able to run. So other people can bear witness to her assaults. Maybe I'll assault her as well. Pound her into the pavement for all she has done. Tomorrow I will be ready. I'm sure of it. Tomorrow I will get the answers I deserve.

35

• • • • •

OPERATION RESCUE – BAD RELIGION

After Dad and I read Mom's latest journal entry, he becomes even more convinced to go to Seattle and find Clarissa. He's baffled that Clarissa could harbor so much resentment, but he does remember that she had a hard time letting go of things. They would get into an argument, and she would stay miffed days later, even after he'd already forgotten what they fought about.

"But almost two decades later?" he asks, rubbing his temples. "Do you think she's still after your mom?"

I shrug. I don't know what to believe anymore. There aren't any entries left in the journal before the pages become blank, so we can't use that as a guide anymore. It's a four-hour-and-change trip to Seattle, and I'm eager to get there so I drive. Dad mans the music selection. Settles on Bad Religion's "Operation Rescue".

"A little too on the nose?" he asks.

We make it by lunchtime, stop to have crab cake sandwiches at this chill spot by the Waterfront. Clarissa doesn't live too far away.

"So, we just go up to her house?" he asks, wiping Old Bay dust from the corner of his mouth. "What do we say?"

"Have you been stalking my mom, lady?"

"This is gonna be a disaster."

It's raining out, typical Seattle. Even when it stops for a minute, the sky looks ominous. I'd only been once before as a little girl. Dad took me and I remember going to the top of the Space Needle. Mom had come back into town for a minute and then proceeded to vanish again. I think he took me to take my mind off her.

"Ready Freddy?" I say. He looks even more freaked out than I do.

We drive up to Clarissa's place, a sad apartment complex with chipped yellow paint and a rusted gate. It's not like I live in the lap of luxury, but clearly Clarissa's Rockstar dreams haven't come to fruition. We ring a doorbell that seems to die when we push it.

Muffled sounds come from behind the door. It opens with the chain still on as an eye appears in the crack.

"Yeah, what?" a voice asks.

"Uhh…" Dad says, stunned for words.

I step in front. "Hi, are you Clarissa?"

"Yeah. What?"

"I'm Love," I start, but then push my dad up to the crack. "My dad is Evan. Evan Marvin."

"What?"

Her voice sounds spooked.

"Evan…Marvin. You two used to…"

"I know who the hell…" She slams the door shut

and for a second I think that's it, she's royally pissed, but then she unlatches the chain and opens the door again.

I'd seen one picture of Clarissa where the whole band is posing in front of an old VW. She was skinny with punk-ish hair and a scowl. The years have definitely hit her hard. Her skin is pockmarky. Her hair just sits there, not doing anything too interesting, the color off-brown. She's still super skinny, but not in a healthy way, like she can't always remember to eat. A smoking cigarette yellows her index and middle finger. She takes a big suck.

"What the fuck are you doing here?" she asks Evan, and then looks me up and down. "'Scuse my language."

"Hey, Clarissa, I know this is weird," Dad begins.

"Weird. This is hella nuts," she says, and devolves into a coughing fit. "Well, fuck it, come on inside. Lest I think this is all a dream."

"It's not," I say, and push my way in.

The place is dimly lit, blinds drawn. Not a home, more like a random mix of furniture: old couch, TV, some lamps, a bare kitchen, two bedrooms in the distance.

"Can I get you something?" she asks, heading to her fridge. She opens it and it's empty. "Yeah, that's what I figured," she mumbles to herself. "I got tap water?"

"Tap water's fine," Dad says, holding his parched throat.

She turns on the faucet and fills up two glasses with somewhat cloudy water. I make a mental note not to sip. We go over to the couch where a TV tray is set up with a sad little microwave meal of mushy potatoes and what looks like maybe Salisbury steak.

She sits across from us in a recliner. Lights another cigarette.

"Want?" she asks, directing the generic pack at us.

We shake our heads.

"I knew I shouldn't have had that drink earlier," she says, nodding at a vodka bottle on the coffee table. "Because this is messing with my mind right now."

"I'm sorry we just barged in," Dad says, trying to be kind.

She huffs a laugh. "Sorry? *You* Evan Marvin are sorry? Fuck off."

Okay, I realize, this is how it's gonna go.

"Why did you stalk my mom?" I yell, having enough with niceties.

"Do what?"

"My mom, Nico Sullivan. You stalked her?"

She chooses not to answer me and ashes her cigarette.

"Evan, I don't hear from you in...what seventeen years? Seventeen years, I think. And you just show up and excuse me of...what again?"

"You didn't answer my question," I say.

"Sweetie, I don't understand what the fuck your question is."

"My mom had a stalker, okay? Someone who followed her around in the shadows. She thought it was you."

She takes another long suck. "You really made something of yourself without me, Evan. First with Grenade Bouquets. I remember watching MTV and seeing you interviewed by Daisy Fuentes. Daisy Fucking Fuentes asking your ass questions—well, really Nico's ass. She was always the star. And then you guys all fell apart and I'm like, 'see, you needed me in the band, you all couldn't make it on your own', and then the two of you form this super band, Evanico, and your album is…everywhere. I can't tell you what that did to me."

Her hand with the cigarette trembles. She's so guilty, I can see it in her eyes. The deception!

"I deserved that success—"

"But you never found it, right," I say. "So you had to make my mom's life a living hell."

She laughs, but it comes out like a cough. "No, no, I mean, a few times I stood outside of your place back in Eugene. Watched you, I dunno. It's not like I loved you, Evan. I wasn't jealous in that way. It was more—I deserved that life, the fame, the fortune."

"The fortune didn't really last," Dad says.

I glare at him and then turn my ire toward her. "So you did stalk her? You admit it?"

"Once or twice like I said, but that was years ago, and seriously, I swear to God, I didn't do it more than twice. I felt—well, I felt pretty lame doing it. For my own sanity, I needed to forget about Nico Sullivan completely. And I did, I mean, I have."

"She writes about you stalking her a lot more than that. She had to go to a clinic. She left the country."

Clarissa holds up her hand. "Now, your mom had issues. Hello, she attacked me on stage—twice! She had zero control. I will take the blame for what I said I did. I stood outside your house, twice, just twice. And then I moved the hell on. I came to Seattle; I was working at a gym. Hell, I'm still doing that. I have a little girl, her father is an ass and out of the picture, so I work. I'm a good mom. She's at sleepaway camp now. This is first summer she went, and I'm having a hard time without her around, so I have a drink, or two, it's no big deal…"

She stops, dabs her finger under her eye to catch a tear.

"I'm feeling very triggered right now."

"Triggered?" I ask.

"Yes, triggered. Your mother did a number on me, you as well, Evan. And just seeing you."

She leaps up and then shoos us to do the same.

"In fact, I think you should go."

"Clarissa, I'm sorry—" Dad begins to say.

She blocks her ears like a child and stamps her foot. "Go!"

Well, you don't need to tell us twice. Dad's still throwing out sorrys, but I'm not apologizing. Even though her life was a shambles, I don't feel bad. She still stalked my mom, got her all crazy. She's to blame.

She's pushing us toward the door and Dad's going on and on about how they were young and didn't know any better, but she's still blocking her ears. It's nuts how things from when you were a teenager could affect you as an adult, like time never passes. It happened to my mom, and it's happening to Clarissa right now.

Once we're outside, we take a second to absorb what occurred.

"That was insane," Dad says, and I nod, pat him on the back.

"She did admit it," I say.

"Yeah, but how does that explain your mom thinking she was still being followed? Unless it was all in her mind."

We sigh because this is the worst case scenario we both fear.

Back in the car, the music turns on with Dad behind the wheel, but I don't want to hear music for once. I'm seriously bummed.

"I'm sorry I dragged you all the way to Seattle," I say.

The rain has stopped, a pinch of sun piercing through a cloud.

"Do you think she's here?" I ask.

He grips the wheel. "If she is, there's only one place I can imagine she'd be."

"Where's that?"

"Flag Pavilion," he says. "Where they had the memorial for Kurt Cobain, almost twenty years ago. I've never been able to return to it after all this time, but maybe she has. For some kind of closure, I don't know."

"It's worth a shot," I say, curious to see it for myself because of my own love for Cobain.

Like mother, like daughter.

He puts the car in the drive and we're off, headed to our last possible hope.

All of our fingers and toes desperately crossed.

36

• • • • •

VANISH ME – LOVE MARVIN

Flag Pavilion had been rebranded as Fisher Pavilion. Flag poles no longer decorate the plaza in front of the pavilion, according to Dad. A circular lawn stands before us: two kids throwing a Frisbee, a few other people hanging out. No sign of Mom.

"We gave it a try," I say, but Dad shakes his head.

"I'm not ready to leave."

He wanders off and I respect his space. He'd been here almost two decades ago with my mom and the rest of Grenade Bouquets after they lost their hero. There had to be some heavy emotions stirring up.

I sit on the grass and take out her notebook. There are no more entries. I get out a pen and decide to add one of my own, but instead of journaling, what comes out is a song. One that has been marinating in my head this entire time.

VANISH ME
by Love Marvin

You became lost
And so did I
Because you vanished
Forever I cry
I held you back
I robbed your youth
You robbed mine too
Tell you the truth
Vanish me
You long to disappear
Vanish me
It's what I fear
Vanish me
To the moon
Vanish me
Come back soon
A shadow followed
Your mind slipped away
They called me a Ghost
They won't today
You had success
And you had Love, me
I've found my voice
Ready for all to see
Vanish me
You long to disappear
Vanish me
It's what I fear
Vanish me

To the moon
Vanish me
Come back soon
I've hated you
I've loved you
I've lost you
I've mourned
It wasn't till you left
I learned I'm strong
Hope you reappear
Hope we start fresh
Wherever you are
Here at home is best
Vanish me
You long to disappear
Vanish me
It's what I fear
Vanish me
To the moon
Vanish me
Come back soon
I'm waiting
I'm longing
To see you
See you
Again
Love, Love

I put down my pen after feeling like I've left my body. I don't know where I went when I wrote this, but I was gone. I remember nothing. Reading over my words as a chill gooses my body. These words with power. These words with might. So true and raw and real. *If I ever see you again, I will show you*, I think. I promise.

And then, I look up from my pages and far down the pavilion I see a woman on the other side. Is it a ghost? She could be you, barefoot in the grass in her summer dress. Bangles and necklaces. Spiraling curly hair. Have I wanted you to appear so bad that I've animated you? Your ghost won't be enough. Give me the real deal or nothing at all.

I rub my eyes. I want you gone if you're gonna be cruel like this. But then I see Dad from far away staring at you as well. Gawking. No two people could see the same ghost, so you can't be a vision.

I stand up, the journal close to my chest, the last remnant of the old you. Each step is weighted, like I'm walking through water. You're so far away. I pick up my pace, start to run, and you notice, you pivot, your face slightly turned toward mine. Shock hovering at the corner of your lips, in your wide diamond eyes. You're smiling, you're crying. You reach out.

I stop right in front of you, breathing so heavy, thinking I'm having a heart attack. We stand there, breathing each other's sorrow, not ready to speak for eons until you finally do.

"Love," you say. "Love."

Hearing you say my name, after all these fruitless searches, brings me to my knees.

The heavens open up and it pours.

37

. . . . .

LITHIUM – NIRVANA

It's raining so hard we can barely see each other through the downpour. I have a million things to say, but my tongue's not working. There's a little café off to the side, and Dad points that way with his hitchhiker's thumb. My mom's in front of me and I want to reach out to make sure she's still real because I don't believe it. In the café, we dry off, shivering because the AC is pumping. She tells us she'll grab coffees and we find a table in the corner. There's a piece of gum under my seat and I'm picking at it to give myself something to do. Dad rests his chin on his fist in a thinker's pose, Mom in his line of sight.

"I don't know what to say to her," he says, exactly how I feel.

She put us through hell, and we're angry. I wonder if any excuse will change my mind. But the fact that she couldn't let us know she was okay, that's just cruel. When she comes back with the coffees, I angle my chair away from her, uninterested now.

"Picked the wrong day to wear a white dress," she laughs, like it's all a joke, indicating her soaked chest. "Love, I got extra whipped cream on yours. I know you like whipped cream."

Do I? Had we ever spoken about my love for whipped cream? I can't even remember. I take it, our hands briefly touching, and put it to my lips. Take a long foamy sip. I place it down next to her journal, smeared from the rain. Her eyes catch it.

"Oh," she says. She makes a gesture to hand it over to her, but I feel like it's mine now. Especially since I'm such a huge part of the entries.

"Did you read it?" she asks, with a twirl of her hair. I'm not sure if her eyes are glassy because she's on something, or if it's the rain.

"Did you leave it for me?" I ask, the first thing I've said to her.

She cocks her head to the side. "Last time I saw it I was probably twenty-one." She cackles, her bangles jangling as she takes a sip.

"What the fuck is wrong with you?" I shout. Heads whip over. Dad puts his face in his hands. Her smile cracks.

"What?" she asks, giving a confused face.

"Love," Dad says, reaching for my hand. I swipe it away.

"No. No, she's laughing. What are you laughing about? What the fuck could be funny?"

"I-I'm nervous, baby. You make me nervous."

"*I* make you nervous?"

"I don't know what to say?" She turns to Dad to save the situation.

"We've been concerned about you," he says. "You vanished."

"Vanished?" There's that cackle again, her throat raspy. "No, I was traveling."

"You haven't been in contact," I snap.

She throws up her hands. "I had no phone. Seriously, my phone got cut off and I was in an Ashram."

"An Ashram?"

"Mmm hmm, in Nepal. Shanti Shivalaya in Butwal. I'd just been through a break-up, and I don't know, needed an Eat, Pray, Love trip with the emphasis on Pray. I did a lot of praying. Soul-searching. Spelunking."

I turn to Dad like *Is she fucking kidding us right now?* We shed tears. We lost sleep. And she was in Nepal praying? It's a joke.

"I had a break-up," she says. "A bad, bad break-up. He was one of those star fucker types." She sucks at her lips. "Cleaned out my account. Well, had enough left for a ticket to Nepal. And things in Nice were becoming stale."

"What about Grandpa Peter?" I ask, and she looks at me like I have three heads.

"Annette said he was doing fine. Responding well to treatments."

"He's in a wheelchair," I say.

"You saw him?"

"Yes," I shout again. "I went to L.A. to see *everyone* from your past trying to get a clue where you'd gone. We thought you were being stalked."

"Evan, really?" Mom asks, making a screwy face.

"Love said you wrote about it in your journal."

Mom eyes the journal. "Sure, maybe almost twenty

years ago. Yeah, I had a thing where I thought I was being followed. I even thought it was Clarissa. Remember Clarissa?"

"Of course, we do," I say. "We came here to see her. We thought she was still after you!"

"That's just nuts. Nuts."

"Are you fucking high right now?" I ask.

"What?"

"Love—" Dad tries to say.

I punch the table with my fist. "Are. You. High. Right. Now?"

"I...I may have had a tiny, tiny bit of pot—"

I jump up and slam my chair into the table. "I can't take this."

I'm running out of the café into the rain. It's coming down even harder. I'm an entity of pure rage. At any moment I can explode. I'm crying and don't know the difference between my tears and the rain on my cheeks.

"Love," I hear and turn around. She's huddled under the awning. "Come here, please come here."

I sigh and stomp over.

"Oh, my sweet baby," she says. "Look at you. So beautiful."

"Stop."

She paws at my hair. "Love the short 'do. Stunning. A woman. You're becoming a woman."

I narrow my eyes. "What do you know of it?"

"Not much to tell you the truth." She nods, forcing a smile until it falls apart. "Not much."

"That's your choice."

She reaches in her purse and takes out a cigarette to light. "You're right. I'm unfit. Always have been."

"Yeah, I read about how much a mistake I was in your journal."

"Those were the ravings of a mad, dumb girl. A girl on lithium half the time, that's what they prescribed me then."

I think of the song "Lithium" by Nirvana. *I love you I'm not gonna crack...*

"I was seeing shadows and... yeah that was a rough time. But a mistake? No, sweetness, you were never a mistake. I'm the mistake."

"You're the mom. Why couldn't you just be a mom?"

"I don't know," she says, sounding so small and defeated. "I'm untethered. I can't stay in one place. I can't do just one thing. The prescribed things we all are supposed to do. Get married. Have a family. Live in a house. It's constricting to me, you see? Relationships are constricting to me."

"I'm not a relationship, I'm your daughter! You don't get to decide to leave."

She blows a trail of smoke. "It's a balancing act."

"What are you talking about?"

"My psyche, my well-being. It's fragile. Any little thing can crack it. You don't want me around when it cracks."

"You had postpartum after I was born," I say.

"Yes, and it never was diagnosed. But I'd had issues before, honey. Even before my sister, Kristen died. Nowadays they might've nipped it in the bud early. We're so much more sensitive to mental health. Back then, it was *verboten*. Teachers, parents, no one wanted to admit defeat like that."

"Aren't you on medication or whatever now?"

She shrugs. "It's not a simple fix. And Western medicine has not always agreed with me. It's made it worse in fact. So, I'm working with an Eastern doctor. It's an ever-evolving process."

"But why couldn't you have just let us know where you were going?"

"I didn't think you cared."

I want to slap her right there.

"You are my mom, of course I care. We've been to hell and back trying to find you."

"I never know where I fit in this family. Your father keeps you at a distance from me."

As if he knows he's being spoken about, he comes out the café.

"Do *not* blame him," I yell. "This is all on you."

She holds up her palms. "You're right. Totally unfair of me. Your father..." She looks at Dad. "Evan is a perfect parent. He's perfect in every way really. It's part of the difficulty in being around him. And so, sometimes it all becomes too overwhelming for me, and I have to jet. That's never gonna change, Love."

It's like a cannonball has been shot into my stomach.

"What are you doing in Seattle?" Evan asks.

"Umm...I dunno. Reliving my youth. Saying hi to Cobain. Drinking some great coffee." She holds up her cup.

I knock the to-go cup out of her hands. "Stop making jokes. It's not funny. I cried over you. I thought you could be dead. Or that you just didn't care. You broke my heart."

She tries to hug me, but I push her away.

"Baby…"

"No, don't baby me. A hug won't make this all better."

"But it never makes it worse. Come, come to mom."

She opens her arms, and after all this time, I can't resist. She smells of cinnamon and cloves. I lean my chin on her shoulder, let forth a gushing of tears I can't contain. When I'm all cried out, she finally lets go.

"I receive what you are saying, Love," she says, looking into my eyes. "This may sound crazy at thirty-four years old, but I have a lot of growing up to do. And this is what I was praying on—what the next stage of my life will be. Maybe less roaming, maybe more permanence?"

I sniffle. "Really?"

She takes my face in her hands. "I'm sorry," she says. "Very, very sorry. To you both. For any hurt I've caused. I'm just trying to fix myself, ya-know. You got caught in the crosshairs, you always have, and that's not fair. If I were you, I'd claw out my eyes. I deserve that."

"Well, maybe not *that*."

She smiles again. "What if I came back to Eugene with you both? Got a place for a minute, stayed a while, made sure my meds were right after all this time in Nepal? Maybe I'll go to L.A. next to see my parents, do an apology tour. Really. It's summer, right? Lots of summer left. What if I gave you this summer, Love? To try and make things right?"

My mind is spinning. I don't want to give in so easily to her, but how much can I yell, and kick, and fight? She's already beaten and I'm exhausted.

I wipe my eyes. "Yeah, whatever, maybe."

"Okay, okay, whatever, maybe. I'll take that. Hey, Ev."

He lifts up his head.

"Will you take that too? Let me hang around Café Hey for a sec?"

He shoves his hands in his pockets. "It's not up to me."

So she glances my way, her eyes begging. I hold all the power for once. I picture a summer where a new relationship blossoms between us. Maybe not mother, daughter. Maybe more like friends, sisters.

And then there's another vision of her leaving again, just when I'd get close and think she'd be here to stay. I can't chance it.

"No," I say.

"No?" she and Dad say together.

"I'm always gonna be worrying that you'll leave." I'm pulling at my sleeves; I'm trying not to cry again.

"I understand," she says, not what I want to hear. And Dad looks like he'll murder her. "I might leave. But I might stay. I live in the moment, Love."

"And where has that gotten you?" I snap. "What do you have to show for that?"

"Experiences," she says, proud.

"Experiences at the detriment of me. Of us. Of a family. A career. A home."

"Those are constructs. Love, you'll have to take me as I am. And I might change. We all change. You've changed since I saw you last. You used to be so quiet, I'd have to pull conversations out of you. But you've found your voice. I can feel its power."

I can't deny that makes me feel good to hear. That she's noticed and what I've been thinking about myself is true. I'm not the same girl I was before she vanished.

"Give me a chance," she says. "And we won't force it with expectations. Natural. Organic. I might surprise you."

"And if you don't?"

"Then I don't. And you can label me a villain. I'm not doing this to make up for what I've done. I'm doing it because I want to. Because you're a kick-ass girl, and I want to hear about everything going on in your life. The good, the bad, and the ugly. Like, is there a boy?"

I chew on the inside of my cheek. "A girl. Maybe."

Dad's eyebrows raise. "A girl?"

"I wanna hear all about this wonderful girl who stole your heart."

I kick at a puddle. "I don't know if she stole my heart."

But I'm as red as a tomato. She loops her arm in mine.

"Give me a chance, Love. Please. Not for me, for you."

I want to believe her. That not only can people change, but they can change for the better. She's so hopeful, a burst of energy.

"Okay," I say, even though the pit of my stomach is heavy as a brick. "Okay."

"Okay," she repeats, locked into an agreement.

Don't let me down, I whisper under my breath. Her ear angles toward my words. She nods. This is her last shot, and I can see the fear in her wild eyes.

38

• • • • •

NEARLY LOST YOU – SCREAMING TREES

Mom found an apartment in West Eugene, not far from where we lived in Friendly. I could bike over in no time at all. It was weird at first, I'm not gonna lie. Sometimes she slept until after noon, so I'd show up with breakfast sammies from Nutton's down the road and no one would answer the door. Nights were when she "shined", as she'd say, so I started heading over after my shifts at Café Hey instead (Dad got me a job again there). I'd get out around nine and meet in her backyard where she'd be listening to music usually, writing songs all day, preparing her voice for when she'd ever sing again.

Early on, we were cautious around one another. I tiptoed, not wanting to give her any reason to leave, and she'd be ultra-careful not to say something that would set me off. But after about a week, we got more comfortable. She'd have a CD going—staying old-school—and we'd just listen. I didn't tell her about writing my own song yet called "Vanish Me". I was enjoying getting to know her for the very first time.

I learned her meds sometimes were uppers and other times downers. "It's my body chemistry for the day," she'd say, with a laissez-faire attitude, accepting this plight. To get off the meds could bring forth horrors unknown.

She wore similar clothes each time: roomy dresses with floral patterns, so much jewelry it made your eyes dance. Feathers and flowers in her hair, a bounty of curls slightly going gray at the ends. "I'm embracing it," she would say. "Middle age, I'm ready for you."

She told me about her past. Filled in the gaps from when her journal ended. How she stayed throughout Europe mostly, had many lovers but none of them stuck. "None of them were your dad," she said, slightly sad. "But they were adventures." How sometimes when the muse struck her right, she'd find a stage and let out her soul. Bathed in the applause.

"But you never wanted to record again?" I asked.

She shook her head. "It stole too much from me. Maybe one day? When I'm stronger. But I'm writing. I'm writing a lot."

She showed me many spiral notebooks. Colored pens filling up the margins. Choruses and verses.

"Some are good, some are horrible. But it's been so long since I've put pen to paper."

Under the humid sky, we'd listen to her favorites, her idols, her reason for being: Hole and Nirvana, not just the popular songs, Pearl Jam and Stone Temple Pilots, Soundgarden and Alice in Chains, Smashing Pumpkins, Temple of the Dog, L7 and the Cranberries, and then even her Lilith Fair years: Jewel and Sarah

McLachlan, Joan Osborne and Fiona Apple. She was still in touch with Jewel, called her a friend for life, a few times escaping to her ranch and riding horses when her demons were at their worst, when they poked and prodded the most.

I told her about Frankie and Caden. How I loved Frankie, but she didn't love me back in that way. How Frankie couldn't love anyone in that way and Caden was the same.

"Maybe they're perfect for each other then?" she said. "Sex has a way of muddling up a relationship big time."

I hadn't seen Frankie and Caden as much in those weeks, busy with Mom. We talked a bit, and I knew they were hanging out with each other a lot. I wanted to be respectful. If I couldn't have Frankie, I couldn't think of anyone else but Caden that deserved her. But between work and my mom, there was really no time for much else.

She'd ask about Dad a lot. Whether he was happy or not. I told her about Marjorie, who he'd been spending a lot more time with. Sometimes even sleeping over. We'd meet in the mornings, awkwardly bumping into each other over coffee at home and then again at Café Hey if she was bringing over her blondies. But she was sweet and I could see cared about my dad a lot. And he was different with her around too. He no longer sang "Nothingman" in the shower or plucked his guitar sadly at night when he thought no one was listening.

Mom was very curious about Delilah too. Being Winter's daughter, she found it fascinating that we were "dating", although I don't know if I'd actually call it that. We talked a lot on the phone, but I started to want to see her face, so Dad got me my first smart phone. I know, crazy. I swore to myself I would never use social media and it was purely to see Delilah when we talked. Since Mom took up my time at night, I'd talk to Delilah in the mornings after I woke up. We'd talk about anything and everything. She was still staying at her Gram's for the summer, and I'd hear about Edina being batshit and playing 60's music really loud. Still, it was good for to her to have a break from her mom for a minute.

As the weeks went on, this all became routine, but a sharp stone sat in my throat for what would happen when summer would end. I knew Mom wouldn't stay in Eugene forever. She spoke about wanting to see my grandparents down in L.A. and all of her old friends. I worried that once she went to L.A., she'd wind up staying, or heading somewhere even farther. But I avoided bringing it up, and so the days turned uber hot as August rolled around, the two us sweltering under the Oregon sky each night.

We're listening to the Screaming Trees' "Nearly Lost You" when she lowers the music, two solitary tears trickling down her cheeks.

"What's wrong?" I ask, getting nervous.

"Nothing." She shakes her head. "I'm happy."

"Me too, me too."

We avoided even talking about our past. How she wasn't there for me when I needed her most. What's the point of rehashing old wounds? But I could see it still ate at her.

"I was such a shit," she says. "Such a fucking shit."

"No," I say, but she really was.

She gives me a look like I can't fool her. "You can say it, Love. I was a fucking shit."

"Fine, you were a fucking shit."

She breathes in this truth. It seems to enliven her. "I can never tell you how sorry I am."

"No," I say, and think on it a second. "But that's okay. We're starting new with this summer."

I know this is naïve. That we've created a Band-Aid, and in the future, it'd rip off. I'd have at her. But not now. Let me have this one perfect summer.

"I'm getting antsy, baby," she says, ashamed.

I sit up, the butterflies in my stomach raging. "What do you mean?"

"Not with you," she says, waving her palms. "Not with this. Our special nights. But of Eugene. The sameness of it all."

"Okay."

"It's time for me to go to L.A."

"Okay."

"But you can come if you want?"

I don't expect this offer.

"What do you mean?"

"I was looking at places. Probably should be close to your grandpa. So maybe Los Feliz, or Glendale is more what I can afford. We could get a place."

"I…have school. I mean, it starts in a few weeks."

"You can come till then. I was talking to Jeremy, and he knows a club manager who was interested in me singing."

"Really? Singing?"

"Yeah, Love, I think I'm ready. And L.A. is where I

know the most people. I have the best support system. I have you here, but it's lonely during the days."

"Oh, I didn't realize."

"And it will be even more when you go back to school. You'll be busy with school, your friends, homework."

I give her a look that says, Love doesn't really do homework.

"You're a lot like I was back then, but I want you to go to college, get your grades up. Do what I wasn't able to do." She spins a curl of hair around her finger. "You could see Delilah if you come to L.A."

"Yeah, it's been weeks since we saw each other in person."

"I've already asked your dad."

"Shut up, really?"

"He wants you to go. Until school starts of course. And it would mean a lot to me if you would. Can you handle us being roommates? Will you wanna rip my head off?"

This is a dream, I think. I want to pinch myself.

"Okay," I say, trying not to gush and show my excitement. I dig into my pocket and pull out the song I wrote about her – "Vanish Me".

"What's this?" she asks, taking it from my hands.

I shrug. "A song I wrote."

"Vanish Me?" she asks, her tight mouth indicating she know what this is about, the melancholy in her eyes. "It's about me, isn't it?"

I nod.

"Can I read it when I'm alone?" she asks. "It might be hard to do so with you here."

I'm scared for her to have it, as if it could alter all the wonder we've created between us this summer.

"Why don't you go home and pack? I can get plane tickets for us tomorrow?"

"Okay."

"Goodnight, Love," she says, clutching it close to her chest like I did with her journal, which had been a window into herself.

Now it's time for her to open the window into me.

39

• • • • •

BONUS TRACK
RUNAWAY TRAIN – NICO SULLIVAN

After a month in L.A., I have to head back to Eugene tomorrow before school starts. I'm definitely not ready to leave. Mom and I rented a place in Los Feliz near my grandpa, and we spent a lot of time with him, Annette, and Grandma Luanne and Roger too. I'd *never* seen my grandparents together, but once a week, Grandpa Peter hosted a catered dinner in his magnificent backyard. They were always cool with each other, never super friendly, but respected Mom and I enough to remain civil. It seemed like her relationship with them had gotten better over the month too. Certainly not perfect, but honestly, what relationships are perfect? I think they all learned to let go of any resentment and start fresh. It was a recipe that Mom and I followed as well.

In fact, I started calling her Nico because we didn't quite fit as mother and daughter. We were more like great roommates. I encouraged her to sing again, and she booked herself a show at this place Electric that

Jeremy recommended. His boyfriend Lo had an in, and let's be truthful, who *wouldn't* wanna see Nico Sullivan perform after all these years? But Nico wanted the guest list kept to a minimum—just friends and family. If it went well, she'd branch out.

So, she spent a lot of time practicing her old songs. Some from Grenade Bouquets and others from Evanico, along with her favorite covers: "Violet" by Hole, Nirvana's "Smells Like Teen Spirit", Ace of Base's "The Sign" dedicated to her sister Kristen, and of course, "Runaway Train" by Soul Asylum. That song had been playing on the radio in her car when she took off from L.A. at sixteen and her life changed. So it held a super special place in her heart.

She never mentioned the song I wrote—"Vanish Me", but I tried not to be upset. I figured the lyrics cut a little too close to home, and it was easier to pretend like it never existed. There'd be other songs I could write that I'd show her in the future, maybe ones that didn't hold such a clear mirror up to her face.

I found L.A. inspiring and wrote a lot in my journal. Most of the songs terrible, but a few had potential. Regardless, it felt great to put my ideas to paper, and I knew they would be the start of many.

When Nico wasn't practicing or seeing my grandparents, she spent a lot of time with Jeremy and Lo. They would come over and Jeremy would tell me stories from when she was young. She was such a wild child. It's hard to believe we're even related. But I like to think of it as opposites attracting. And music does tie us together. It always will.

The other great thing about L.A. was Delilah.

Sometimes Nico and Winter would hang with me and Delilah. We'd go out to restaurants, or Winter took us to concerts or an art show as our official tour guide to L.A. Other times, Delilah and I would do things on our own. She didn't have many local friends, so I didn't have to share her with anyone. We'd go hiking in Griffith Park or laze around the pool at the apartment complex we were renting. We still only kissed—and we did a *lot* of kissing. I wasn't ready to do more yet and she was cool with that. We made plans for her to fly to Eugene Columbus Day weekend. But I knew it be hard to leave her till then. A long-distance relationship wouldn't be easy.

For Nico's show, she invited Dad and Marjorie. They agreed to come, and I was really excited because I'd never gone this long without seeing Dad and I missed him a lot. I even got Frankie and Caden to take the trip again. Caden's moms hadn't been on a vacation forever, so they agreed to bring Frankie as well and stay in a hotel in Beverly Hills. Everyone would be coming to the show.

When I arrive at Electric, I have nervous butterflies, which is strange because I'm not the one singing. I'm scared for Nico. She's put so much effort into this show, and I want it to be amazing for her. She deserves it. Her meds seem to be evening out, and she's been really good about not having too much alcohol or drugs. I know that a great set will help her stay down that road.

"Hey," Delilah says, bumping my hip when I arrive. She's dressed in a plaid skirt with a Ramones tee and her hair tied in pigtails. We kiss and her lips taste like peaches. "Don't be nervous," she says, because I'm picking at my nails.

"I didn't see her this morning when I woke," I say. "She came right here."

"She's gonna do fine. Winter's been with her."

"They've been getting along so well."

"I know! It's really boosted Winter's spirits. I think she really missed her as a friend." Delilah waves across the room. "There's Uncle Jeremy."

Jeremy and Lo come over, both wearing purple faux fur coats that remind of Grimace from the McDonalds gang.

"Isn't this place the tits?" Lo says, surveying the scene. It has a retro kitsch vibe. 50's televisions on the wall, Coca-Cola neon signs, Cheshire Cat clocks. "It's new, but I think Nico can put it on the map."

"If anyone can put a place on the map, it's Nico," Jeremy says, snapping his fingers in Z formation. "And how are my little lovebirds?" he asks, hugging me and Delilah.

"Stop," she says.

"Yeah, seriously stop," I add.

"So cute, you two could be on top of a cake."

"Speaking of cake," Lo says, "I need to get some food in me, even if it's just bar nuts."

"He gets hangry," Jeremy says. Lo rolls his eyes and saunters off. "And how's Nico?"

"I haven't seen her yet this morning," I say, and he looks grim.

"I'm sure she's fine."

"Everyone keeps saying that," I say.

Jeremy claps. "Well, then it's the truth." He claps again. "OMG, it's your little friends."

Frankie and Caden enter along with Caden's moms. I burst away from everyone and give them both a strangling hug, never spending this long away from *9021-Hole*. Frankie and I start talking over one another.

"Your hair," I say, because she's dyed it bright blue, Caden too.

"Yeah, we're trying it out…together."

They hold hands. Caden's smiling. If I think back, I'm not sure I'd ever seen him smiling before. And while it's weird to see them holding hands, I'm truly happy for them.

"You look so L.A.," Frankie says. "You're not pasty!"

I laugh at that. It's true, laying out by the pool has turned my snow-white skin to off-white.

"How's your mom doing?" Caden's moms ask at the same time, and then laugh.

"I don't know!" I say, slapping my forehead. "She vanished this morning…" I chew on the words, my stomach getting queasy. What if she vanished again for good? I put this thought out of my head, so I won't drive myself crazy.

"I dig the hair too," Delilah says, coming over and giving Frankie and Caden a friendly hug. She then takes my hand. The four of us stand there facing one another, each couple holding hands. It feels okay. Like this is how it's supposed to be. I think I'm even blushing.

"There's my princess," I hear, and Dad and Marjorie enter too.

"Dad!"

I jump in his arms, and he looks a little older, the gray in his beard a little grayer. I stay hugging him for a while.

"Let me look at you," he says, twirling me around. "My L.A. girl, so grown up."

"Stop, Dad," I say, but really want him to keep going.

"You're taller!" he gushes.

"No, I'm not," I say, but I realize I'm up to his chin now. "Wow, maybe I have grown."

"And how's your mother?" he asks.

"I have no idea. She left before I woke up this morning."

He gets worry lines on his forehead, but then he smiles, wiping them away. I know he worried for a second like I did but won't show it.

"Hey, Love," Marjorie says, and comes in for a hug.

"Let me see it," I say.

She shows me her ring finger with a cute diamond. The big news was that Dad proposed last week. Yeah, it's fast, but just looking at their cheesy grins, I could tell it's the right time. The wedding will be a year from now, so there's no rush with that. They want to aim for the end of the end of next summer before I go to college.

Yeah, that's the last bit of news. I decided to get my grades up from god-awful and go to college. I'm actually thinking of Santa Monica college, which is a community college, at least for two years. It'll keep me in L.A. and then I could decide to transfer somewhere else. Right now, Delilah and I are talking about going together, but we know it's a long way off and to just take it day by day.

"Well, look at this gang of partygoers," Winter says,

stepping out from behind the stage. She has on boots that go all the way up her legs, a distressed shirt with slashes in it, blue eye shadow, feathered hair and a red, red lip. "The star is about to emerge. Time for everyone to find their seats."

Delilah and I grab stools by a bar up close with a perfect view. The lights dim. A huge strobe light shines on the center stage and Nico emerges. She's breathtaking. Her hair blonde and swooped across one eye, leather pants with pointy boots and a leopard print shirt. She takes the microphone in her hands, assesses the crowd.

We're all clapping, but she gestures for us to stop. She takes a deep breath.

"I wanna thank everyone for coming." She's smiling, a true one that stretches up her face. "This has been a long time in the making, but great things come to those who wait, a cliché, yeah, yeah. Anyway, my true love has always been music. Music has helped me during my lowest of lowest, it's been a part of my highest of highs, but nothing compares to the important people in my life." She catches a tear with a sharp fingernail. "My beautiful friends, who I've known for over two decades." She shakes her head in awe at Winter and Jeremy, who do the same. "The very best baby daddy on the planet, my brilliant ex Evan..." She winks at Dad, who winks back. "Congrats on your engagement. Marjorie's a lucky, lucky soul." I feel her gaze turn to me. "And finally, my true, true love on this planet, my little girl, my own Love, who's now becoming a woman. This is for you, baby."

She launches into Hole's "Violet", not thrashing and

angry like I would expect from that song, but quiet and soulful. She sings to the heavens. She follows that up with "Smells Like Teen Spirit", in an acoustic set that gives me goosebumps. Next up is "The Sign", which she dedicates to Kristen, "a beautiful energy taken too soon." She sits crossed-legged on the stage for that one, her voice soft, but we're all rapt.

"This next song is one that means a lot to me. I was a very, very lost girl when I was sixteen and I ran away, but I always had this song with me along for the ride. This is 'Runaway Train'."

I'm singing along with her. As she belts out the chorus about being in too deep with no way out and asking how on Earth did she get so jaded, she's a presence on the stage, flailing out, feeling the spirit of the song. She's a bird in flight, she's a woman exorcised. And I'm clapping, clapping with all my heart to see such raw magnificence.

"And now," she says, "for my last song..." She's looking right at me and I'm eating my heart. "This was written by the purest creature I know, my Love, the true talent in this family. Thank you, baby, for letting me in your world again. For letting me show you how much you mean to me."

She sings "Vanish Me," my words coming to life.

Vanish Me
To the moon
Vanish Me
Come back soon

In this moment, we are invincible, her demons at bay. They may return, this I tell myself, and she may need to vanish again. I will let her. I will let her be Nico, not Mom, because she is a powerful entity outside of being just my mom, and I must learn to share her with the world. She will tour again, she will define herself as a star, she will rise to nuclear heights like she did before. It will never be easy path for her soul. She will always fight the worst parts of herself. But she shines so bright—she's blinding, she's a supernova. She will orbit the moon. And inevitably, she might disappear into the darkness.

But if she does, she will come back soon, again and again, and we'll celebrate the return of this runaway train, we'll cherish the moments she'll stop at our station, on her endless, lovely one-way track.

ACKNOWLEDGMENTS

It's been a pleasure to create Nico and her world for these past few years, but all good things must come to an end. I'm greatly indebted to everyone who has helped bring these books to life. My agent Nat Kimber, who has been a passionate cheerleader of Nico from the start, along with the rest of the Runaway Team at The Rights Factory—Karmen Wells on the film/TV front and Sam Hiyate, who has repped me for a dozen years.

The Wise Wolf team that has brought the Runaway books to their home: Rachel Del Grosso, its fantastic editor who liked the first novel, suggested a second, and was open to a third, along with Kristin Yahner and Tracey Govender. Kat Bedrosian for her astute early reads. Raegan Revord for choosing Runaway Train as her #ReadingWithRaegan monthly pick and filming a great Q&A.

And all the grunge, post-grunge, and other bands who inspired me once again and weaved their way into the plot: The Smashing Pumpkins, Pearl Jam, Better Than Ezra, Cake, Tracey Bonham, Nirvana, Red Hot Chili Peppers, Jewel, Alice in Chains, Hole, 311, Soundgarden, Jeff Buckley, Collective Soul, Rockwell, Joan Baez, Natalie Imbruglia, 4 Non Blondes, The Bangles, Plain White T's, Candlebox, Backstreet Boys, Toad the Wet Sprocket, The B-52s, Screaming Trees, Pixies, Garbage, The Verve, Gin Blossoms, Blind Melon, Guster, Bad Religion. And of course, Soul Asylum's "Runaway Train" that put the bug in my ear to go on this journey and continue along its track. Thank you!.

ABOUT THE AUTHOR

Lee Matthew Goldberg is the author of the novels THE ANCESTOR, THE MENTOR, THE DESIRE CARD, SLOW DOWN and ORANGE CITY. He has been published in multiple languages and nominated for the 2018 Prix du Polar. After graduating with an MFA from the New School, his writing has also appeared in The Millions, Vol. 1 Brooklyn, LitReactor, Monkeybicycle, Fiction Writers Review, Cagibi, Necessary Fiction, the anthology Dirty Boulevard, The Montreal Review, The Adirondack Review, The New Plains Review, Underwood Press and others.

He is the editor-in-chief and co-founder of Fringe, dedicated to publishing fiction that's outside-of-the-box. His pilots and screenplays have been finalists in Script Pipeline, Book Pipeline, Stage 32, We Screenplay, the New York Screenplay, Screencraft, and the Hollywood Screenplay contests. He is the co-curator of The Guerrilla Lit Reading Series and lives in New York City. RUNAWAY TRAIN was his first Young Adult novel.